"So, ... en ... or don't you?"

"Of course I love him!"

"Well, that's one of the things I came back to find out. Now that I know, I guess you and I have nothing more to say to each other." Adam rose and zipped up his jacket. "Have a happy life, Georgia."

"That's just what you did when we broke up. Just turned and walked away without even kissing me goodbye!"

**CATHERINE SPENCER**, once an English teacher, fell into writing through eavesdropping on a conversation about Harlequin romances. Within two months she'd changed careers and sold her first book to Harlequin's British arm, Mills & Boon. She moved to Canada from England thirty years ago and now lives in Vancouver. She is married to a Canadian and has four grown children—two daughters and two sons—plus three dogs and a cat. In her spare time she plays the piano, collects antiques and grows tropical shrubs.

## Books by Catherine Spencer

HARLEQUIN PRESENTS
1406—THE LOVING TOUCH
1587—NATURALLY LOVING
1682—ELEGANT BARBARIAN
1812—THAT MAN CALLAHAN!

HARLEQUIN ROMANCE
3138—WINTER ROSES
3348—LADY BE MINE
3365—SIMPLY THE BEST

# CATHERINE SPENCER

# Three Times a Bride

## Harlequin Books

TORONTO • NEW YORK • LONDON
AMSTERDAM • PARIS • SYDNEY • HAMBURG
STOCKHOLM • ATHENS • TOKYO • MILAN
MADRID • WARSAW • BUDAPEST • AUCKLAND

ISBN 0-373-11842-2

THREE TIMES A BRIDE

First North American Publication 1996.

# PROLOGUE

IF SHE hadn't been so preoccupied with entering the security code and locking the door to the studio before she stepped out into the quiet square, she might have realized sooner that he was waiting just for her. But she was too busy making a mental checklist of all the things she had to do before her wedding day to give much attention to the street.

He emerged from the shadow of the building, a dark and stealthy smudge superimposed on the deeper blackness of the night. Georgia felt his presence before she saw him and knew the raw November wind had nothing to do with the chill of awareness that inched past the fur collar of her coat and shimmied the length of her spine.

Belatedly, she noticed that the moon had disappeared behind rain-filled clouds, offering him anonymity. But she, halfway between the building and her car parked at the curb, was fully revealed in the light spilling from the wrought-iron street lamp. With her high heels and slender build, she was unmistakably a woman, unmistakably alone.

She was not afraid, however. Mildly curious, perhaps, but definitely not afraid. She refused to admit to such a possibility. To do so would negate everything she'd struggled to achieve in the last fifteen months. Like passion and rage and wild, obsessive love, fear shredded a person's soul beyond redemption.

She knew. She was a survivor—but only just, and only because she had divorced herself, firmly and irrevocably, from all those raw emotions capable of inflicting pain with supreme indifference to a person's capacity to bear it.

Refusing to acknowledge him by so much as a glance, she continued toward her car. Whoever he was, the man could not touch her. She was too well-defended, cocooned in the pleasant, fuzzy limbo she had built around herself. If he was a panhandler, he would be very disappointed to learn that she had only about ten dollars in her purse. If he was a mugger after her personal jewelry, he'd get her engagement ring, which was insured. But he could not *touch* her. Nothing could violate her inner self like that, not anymore.

Or so she believed. But five yards from her car, he closed in. She could hear the rustle of his clothing, see the condensed puff of his breath.

It was not his hand reaching out to touch her, or the feel of his fingers closing softly around the nape of her neck that taught her differently. It was the supernatural premonition, as his aura collided with hers, that sent the terror shooting through her veins.

Her breath stopped and so did her heart, albeit briefly. She opened her mouth, praying for the wherewithal to cry for help.

And a voice from the grave said softly, "Don't scream, sweet pea. It's just me."

# CHAPTER ONE

...THEY HAD MET three years before, at the Dog Days of August Dance at the Riverside Club. He'd looked up as she came in from the terrace, brought his smoky-blue gaze to bear on her, and suddenly those corny lyrics from *South Pacific* had made perfect sense. He was a stranger, lounging with narrow-hipped grace against the bar on the other side of the room, chatting with Steven Drake, the most eligible bachelor in town, but when he'd seen Georgia, he'd let the conversation lapse, straightened to his full height, and shrugged his black, open-necked shirt into place on his fabulous shoulders.

Just then, the band switched from a classic 1950's foxtrot to the pulsing beat of *Time of Your Life* from *Dirty Dancing*, and she'd known with fatal certainty that he was going to saunter over, take her hand, and lead her out onto the floor. And that the way he'd dance with her would set staid old Piper Landing on its ear, and that she'd never be the same again.

"How could you?" her sister, Samantha, had squawked the next day. "Everybody's talking about the exhibition you made of yourself with the grandson of that crazy old hippie, Bev Walsh."

"Hardly a hippie, dear," their mother had said with somewhat less vehemence, "But Bohemian, certainly, and eccentric, too. Definitely not someone we care to cultivate."

It couldn't have mattered less to Georgia if he'd been related to Lucrezia Borgia. They'd spent the rest of that first evening together, danced—disgracefully, no doubt—

7

until dawn, barely been able to tear themselves away from each other, and continued to shock local society for the remainder of the time he was in town.

It had been instant romance, complete with every timeless cliché, the only flaw being that he belonged to the United States Air Force and was on leave in Piper Landing for only a week or two.

"You cannot possibly intend to pursue this relationship?" her mother had gasped when Georgia made it plain that her affair with the dashing Lieutenant Colonel Adam Cabot was no passing fancy. "Dear Heaven, Georgia, isn't it time you settled down and remembered who you are?"

That had been yet one more round in an ongoing volley of disapproval over the fact that Georgia had turned up her nose at the chance of a university education, and opted instead to don a leather apron and learn the jewelry business from the bottom up.

"Chamberlaines do not serve apprenticeships," her mother had decreed, upon learning that, at eighteen, her eldest daughter had signed over the next several years of her life to Giovanni Bartoli, the famous designer who worked in Vancouver.

When her father heard she was traveling to places like Colombia, Brazil, South Africa and Thailand in pursuit of her career, he'd been sure she'd end up at the mercy of rebels or bandits or worse. But Georgia had thrived on the experience. Up until the day she'd met Adam, the biggest thrill of her life had been her first solo trip to the diamond exchange in Amsterdam.

"Get married?" she'd scoffed when her parents suggested that, at the ripe old age of twenty-six and with her apprenticeship successfully concluded, she might want to give the matter some thought. "Not likely! I value my independence too much."

"Get married?" her mother had gasped, practically falling victim to a stroke when, a mere two years later, Georgia had announced that she and Adam were engaged. "To that man? You can't be serious, my dear!"

But Georgia had never been more serious in her life, nor had she ever been happier. Sadly, it had all been too good—too volatile—to last.

The shrill summons of the telephone brought her bolt upright from what more properly resembled exhausted collapse than sleep. Groping for the receiver, Georgia squinted blearily at it. Awash with a number of conflicting emotions, she couldn't drum up her usual courteous greeting and managed only to croak furtively, "Yes?"

Her mother's normally well-modulated voice cut the air with the staccato urgency of rifle fire. "Georgia? You're not ill, are you? Ye gods, don't tell me you've come down with something at this late date! Georgia, are you still there? Why don't you say something?"

"I'm here, Mother," Georgia managed, emotions still churning.

"You *are* ill," Natalie accused with woeful certainty. "Oh, Georgia, how could you?"

Georgia would have liked to tell her mother not to get herself into a state but that would have been misleading since, when she heard the news, the mother of the bride would have every reason to be very upset indeed. So Georgia offered a half-truth in the hope that it might buy her a little time. "I'm not ill, Mother."

"Well, you sound like the wrath of God."

"Probably because I'm still half asleep."

"Why? It's almost eight and you never sleep in."

"I did today, Mother. I had a restless night."

"Oh, well, that explains it." Natalie's sigh was full of relief. "Pre-wedding nerves, dear. All brides get them."

*Not like mine*, Georgia could have told her, but decided discretion was the better part of valor at this hour of the morning. She needed to fortify herself with a dose of good strong coffee before she relayed to her mother news that threatened to sabotage yet another wedding planned on her behalf. "I've got a client coming in at ten, Mother, and I really ought to get a move on, so unless there's something in particular you wanted to talk about...?"

"Nothing that can't wait until lunch, dear."

"Lunch?" Georgia's stomach rolled over in protest at the mere thought.

"My goodness, Georgia, you really *are* a nervous bride." Her mother's laughter trilled merrily down the line. "We made the date last week, remember? One o'clock at the Club, just you, me and Samantha, to go over a few last details. We'll pick you up at the studio about half past twelve. Don't keep us waiting."

The abrupt click as the line went dead lent an immediacy to the request that propelled Georgia into action as little else could have done. In her present state, she was in no condition to see anyone, least of all her highly strung, socially correct mother and sister. She needed to pull herself together, fast.

Reeling a little, she sidled past the full-length mirror on her closet door, trying to ignore its mocking reflection of her hollow-eyed face, and headed for the bathroom. Was it possible, she wondered, that if she subjected herself to the pulsing force of the hottest water skin and bone could tolerate, what had happened last night might dissipate into steam and turn out to be nothing more than a very bad dream?

Certainly, it had all the earmarks of make-believe. After all, how many other women found themselves face to face with an ex-fiancé who, believed dead for over a year, showed up very much alive two weeks before his one-time bride's marriage to his best friend? And she *had* fainted dead away at the sight of the apparition, could still feel the lump on her head from when she'd keeled over, which was enough to make anyone hallucinate a little.

But could she possibly have imagined the sound of that voice with its lazy American drawl, or the feel of those arms that had scooped her up and bundled her into the passenger seat of her car? Could anyone other than the real Lieutenant Colonel Adam Cabot, retired—supposedly—U.S. Air Force, have driven her home with such efficient dispatch?

No. That had been no passing stranger playing Good Samaritan. That had been Adam, the man who, in choosing career over love, had driven her to cancel their wedding fifteen months ago and made her the pitied topic of conversation at every dinner party in Piper Landing for most of the time since. And when her mother found out that he was alive and about to wreak havoc in her life a second time, all hell would break loose.

Because havoc he would indeed wreak. He'd made that much plain during the time it had taken him to deposit her, weak-kneed, on her doorstep, last night.

"I realize, Georgia," he'd murmured wryly, casting her a sideways glance as he followed her directions to the house she now lived in, "that the notion of creeping up on you unannounced tonight might have been ill-conceived on my part and that you're understandably shocked, but I can't say I'm especially flattered by your less-than-enthusiastic reaction at seeing me again."

"I'm having trouble believing my eyes," she'd quavered, with a feeble lack of originality. "You don't seem real."

"Oh, I'm real enough," he'd assured her, a trace of his old sexy grin gleaming in the streetlights of Piper Landing's tree-lined crescents, "and if it's proof you're looking for, this ought to do it."

And he'd clamped a warm, very alive and very possessive hand on her knee. She'd shied away from the contact and almost squealed with fright.

He'd noticed. He'd withdrawn his hand and when he spoke again, that sexy drawl had taken on a distinctly caustic edge. "Sorry you're not happier to see me," he said.

"I don't quite know what you expect me to say," she'd replied defensively.

"How about, 'Gee, honey, what took you so long to show up?' Or, 'What's a nice ghost like you doing in a town like this?'"

"Are you a ghost?" she'd whispered, with a mixture of dread and hope.

"Not on your life, Georgia. I'm the real thing, and turning your lovely face away won't make me disappear, no matter how much you might wish it would."

Nor had it. He'd shifted in the driver's seat, angling himself so that he could watch her and the road at the same time. Steering with casual, one-handed skill, he'd pushed back a lock of her blond hair and secured it behind her ear, leaving her profile exposed and vulnerable. "You've grown your hair long," he remarked.

"Not long," she'd muttered, swinging her head away. "Just longer than I used to wear it."

"It changes you, makes you less...vibrant."

She'd felt his gaze on her, sharply observant. "Turn left at the next intersection," she said, "and keep your eyes on the road. I don't want to end up in the ditch."

But what she really meant was, *Stop trying to look inside me. There's nothing there anymore.*

It was true. Losing him had left her heart so impoverished it could barely function. Oh, it pumped out its daily quota of blood all right, but the real heart was gone and left a space where the true love of her life had once lived.

"This is a far cry from your old place," he'd said, slowing down for the approach to her house. "Practically country, from the looks of it. What made you decide to move out of the apartment?"

She didn't bother explaining that she'd wanted to leave behind everything associated with him because remembering was too painful. Instead, she leapt from the car as fast as her still-trembling legs could carry her, anxious to put as much distance between him and her as possible.

He'd sensed her aversion and had dropped her car keys into her hand with curt formality. "I know we didn't part on the most loving of terms," he said, "but I had hoped you'd since found it in your jealous, insecure little heart to get over your pique. Apparently I was wrong."

"I'm sorry," she'd said, aware that the words were hopelessly inadequate. "I'm too dazed to know how I feel or what I should be saying."

"So it seems." He'd shrugged and looked around at her house and its winter-bare garden that sloped down to the river. "Do you mind phoning for a taxi? I'm not sure where we are exactly, but I'd guess it's a bit too far for me to walk back to Bev's place."

"Of course. Would you...do you want to wait inside?"

His gaze had zeroed in on her again with brutal candor. "Yes. I want to see where you live, where you sleep, what you wear in bed, and if you keep my picture on your nightstand."

"Oh...!" She'd quailed at the prospect and with the disquieting insight of an old lover, he'd detected her dismay.

In that bossy way of his that before had always invited her defiance, he'd continued, "But I'll wait to be invited. Get inside, for Pete's sake, and pour yourself a stiff drink. You look as if you could use one. I'll walk back to the service station we passed a mile or so down the road, and call for a taxi from there. We can put off the glad reunion until another time."

She'd been happy to comply. "Thank you!"

The heartfelt relief in her response had sent a grimace skittering over his features. "I said 'put off', sweet pea, not 'forget'. You *will* be seeing me again. We have so much news to catch up on."

Then he'd turned and marched down her driveway, the firm thud of his stride gradually diminishing into silence.

If only he'd chosen to disappear in a puff of smoke...!

Stepping out of the shower, Georgia swathed her hair in a towel and checked the clock on the wall. Eight twenty-five. Four hours, give or take a few minutes, before she met her mother and sister. Four hours in which to digest the reality of Lieutenant Colonel Adam Cabot's resurrection from the dead and make her peace with it.

She had thought herself safe from such upheaval. Had spun a cocoon around herself so intricately woven that she'd been sure nothing could threaten it. Not passion, or hate; not rage, or joy. Just calm affection, subdued pleasure, serene indifference.

She had turned to Steven, her new house, her work—and yes, the thousand and one busy things associated with a wedding that, this time, her family whole-heartedly approved of—hoping these things would be enough to compensate for what she had lost.

Beverley Walsh, Adam's grandmother, had tried to warn her, the day they'd accidentally met downtown about six months after Adam had supposedly died. "It takes two years, foolish child," she'd said, referring to the fact that Georgia and Steven were spending a lot of time together. "After that, although you won't have for-gotten your first love, you will have accepted its loss. Then, and not before, will you be ready to start over with someone else."

Georgia hadn't been able to wait that long; the pain was too crushing, the guilt too severe. It wasn't just the fact of Adam's death, it was knowing she'd sent him to it.

She'd been with him, the day he received the call from his C.O. asking him to postpone his retirement for an extra two months, "just long enough to put this prototype fighter jet through its paces and identify the bugs bothering our other pilots. You can spare me that, can't you?"

"I'm afraid I can't sir. I'm getting married in six weeks," Adam had said, but Georgia had seen the flare of excitement in his eyes, the sudden longing he'd tried to hide, and she'd known that, if it had been up to him alone, he'd have snatched at this last chance to fly the most exciting fighter aircraft yet to leave the drawing boards.

"I think you should go," she'd said, after he'd hung up the phone.

"No. All that's behind me." He'd tried to sound ac-cepting but she'd heard only the regret, the sudden resurgence of uncertainty that had dogged the months before he'd finally reconciled himself to giving up military life and settling down as a civilian.

Sensing this, and because she loved him, she had offered him an escape, manufacturing a reason that had everything to do with what she thought he needed, at the cost of what she desperately wanted: a man she adored for her husband—and a father for the child he did not know she had conceived.

"I'm not sure getting married is such a good idea," she'd said, giving voice to the most barefaced untruth of her life. "I think a cooling-off period might be very good for us."

"Have you lost your mind?" he'd said. "What about the three hundred guests your mother had to invite to the wedding? What about the dress and the veil and all that other paraphernalia?"

"What about the things that really matter to us?" she'd countered, and because they'd once been valid, she was able, with a conviction that left him stunned and angry, to rattle off all the reasons for not going ahead with their wedding.

"Are you trying to tell me you don't love me, Georgia?" he'd asked at last.

To deny that was more lie than she could bring herself to utter. "No—just that I'm not sure either of us loves the other enough to give up our freedom. Let's put the wedding on hold for now and see how we feel when you get back."

It had been a not unreasonable gamble, she'd thought at the time. She'd found out only the day before that she was five weeks pregnant. Once his two month term was up, they'd still have plenty of time to get married before the baby was born.

"I thought we'd decided we couldn't be happy away from each other, Georgia," he'd said, but although his voice had been somber, his eyes had betrayed him. He was behaving like a gentleman when all he really wanted was to be an officer on active duty again.

She hadn't been able to bear it. "Oh, please!" she'd cried. "Just go, and stop pretending it's not what you want, too."

Some of the light had gone out of his eyes at that. "Since you put it so kindly, maybe I will."

"Terrific!" She'd wrenched his ring from her finger and flung it at him. "There, now it's official. The engagement's off until you finally decide you can live without the Air Force. Go and fly your damned toy. Fly it off the edge of the earth if it pleases you!"

He'd caught the ring, deftly tossed it in the air like a coin, and tucked it into the breast pocket of his shirt. "Okay," he'd said flatly.

Then he'd done as she'd asked. Without a touch, a kiss, or another word, he'd turned and left her.

In the dreadful days that followed, she had not known how she would endure the rest of her life without him. But now that he was alive after all, she could have outlasted eternity before having to face him again.

She was not granted more than two hours. Shortly after her ten o'clock clients left the studio, the buzzer at the front entrance sounded. When she peered through the burglar-proof glass double doors fronting onto the street, Adam stood on the other side. Clad in narrow navy jeans, a royal blue turtleneck sweater and a doeskin suede jacket, he looked so thoroughly gorgeous that, for a very little while, all the problems and complications inherent in his reappearance took second place to the sheer miracle and pleasure of being able to look at him again.

He had changed. Was thinner, cut closer to the bone, without sacrificing any of that startling male beauty that had first drawn her to him. His cheekbones carved a more austere angle beneath the smooth, slightly tanned skin, and in the revealing light of day she noticed that his curly black hair was now touched with gray at the temples. His mouth, that used to laugh so easily and often, assumed a severity that was new. But his heavily lashed eyes were exactly as she remembered them, smoky blue and direct, even though the lines fanning from the outer corners were etched more deeply.

A feeling like nothing she'd ever known rolled over Georgia, much like a door that had been firmly locked and bolted suddenly creaking ajar and threatening to release all kinds of demons. It left her panic-stricken. "What do you want?" she asked through the intercom.

"To talk to you, obviously," Adam replied grimly, "though not with me standing out here on the street for all and sundry to hear, so you might as well let me in. You and I do, after all, have rather a lot to say to one another, don't you think? And just because I was gentleman enough last night not to push you into a mutual *exposé* of everything that's befallen us since the last time we saw each other doesn't mean I'm willing to put it off indefinitely."

She could have made excuses; said she had a dental appointment in another country or something, but what was the point? Sooner or later, she'd have to deal with him and time wasn't exactly on her side.

"Some fancy system you've got here," he observed as the electronic device that protected her inventory admitted him through the outer door and then the inner. "When did you become so safety-conscious?"

She blushed a little at the lightly sugared scorn underlying his words. "When it was pointed out to me that my stock makes me a target for theft on a grand scale. Taking precautions seemed the safe and sensible thing to do.''

''*Safe and sensible*? The Georgia I used to know never concerned herself with being either safe or sensible.''

''She changed in the months after...''

''I died?'' He stepped closer, his smile so reminiscent of his old sweet smile that she almost mistook it for the real thing. Almost. ''It's okay, sweet pea,'' he assured her dryly. ''You can say it.''

An absurd, unreasonable guilt made her hide her left hand behind her back. ''It's not okay,'' she blurted out, retreating. ''And you can't call me 'sweet pea', not anymore.''

''Why not?'' His smile didn't slip an inch but she realized now what made it different. It did not touch those blue eyes whose gaze dissected her with such acute, unwavering interest.

''Because...'' She faltered, the words damming up for all that she wished she could let them spill out and be over with.

''Because you're wearing another man's ring?'' He nodded calmly at her startled gasp, and unzipped his suede jacket as if this were just another in a long list of social calls he had to make that day. ''Yes, I know. You're engaged to my best friend, Steven.''

''Who—how did you...?''

''Beverley told me. Who else?''

Georgia sagged against the desk at her back. ''Of course. I should have known.''

Adam lifted his shoulders disbelievingly. ''Did you expect her to keep quiet about it?'' he asked, and she realized that, beneath his composed facade, disgust warred with cold anger. ''She's my grandmother, and very loyal to those she loves—unlike some I could name.''

"I bet she couldn't wait to tell you."

He continued to pin Georgia in that sharp, unforgiving gaze. "She waited over a year. Nearly fifteen months, to be exact, during which time she mourned my apparent death. How did you spend the time, Georgia, my love? Running want ads in the Lonely Hearts column of the Piper Landing *Daily News*? How many poor slobs did you reject before you decided to save yourself a lot of bother and settle for good old Steven, who was so conveniently handy once I'd vacated the scene?"

"It wasn't like that," she said, flushing at the brazen contempt in his tone. "I didn't date anyone, not even Steven at first. But you and he had been friends for years, and he was the only one who really understood what I went through when you—when I thought you were...dead."

"You're wrong. He wasn't the only one. Beverley would have understood, if you'd cared to give her the chance to share whatever small portion of grief you decided I deserved."

There were many things Georgia could have said in retaliation, among them that Beverley Walsh hadn't particularly wanted to share her grandson in life and had been damned if she'd allow anyone to intrude on her sorrow at his death; or that Georgia's own anguish had been so keen that, for a while, it had taken all her strength to face each unrelenting day; or that many had been the time that she'd wished for nothing but an end to her own miserable, guilt-ridden existence, so empty and pointless had it seemed without Adam. But his greatest misconception—that she'd turned easily to another man—was the one she felt most compelled to address.

"Steven was never more your friend than in the days and weeks after you...disappeared. I think *I* would have died without him. He gave me back my sanity when I thought I'd lost it forever. He helped me to accept what I couldn't change and would never understand. And he asked for nothing in return except the solace of sharing memories of you. It's only over the last four or five months that we've...grown closer."

"And how close is that, Georgia?" Adam leaned against a glass presentation cabinet with careless disregard for its fragility. "Close enough that he makes you forget the times you made love with me? Close enough that you cry out his name instead of mine when the passion takes hold? Close enough—"

"Stop it!" Georgia clapped her hands to her ears, her earlier flush a pale imitation of the real thing as a wave of embarrassment and indignation left her face flaming. "It's no longer any of your business!"

"I guess not." His deceptively lazy gaze missed nothing as it swept over the studio's costly display of jewelry before finally coming to rest on her. He stared insolently at her full-skirted silk and cashmere suit, the cameo brooch at her throat, the baroque pearl studs in her ears. And last of all, he looked long and hard at the two carat diamond solitaire engagement ring on her finger. "I guess life goes on, no matter what. Things change, people change. For a thirty-year-old woman, you've achieved impressive success, Georgia. Grief has worked wonders on you."

She rounded on him, stung. "How dare you cheapen how I felt and turn it into something contemptible and shallow?"

He shrugged, his shoulders lifting easily under the supple doeskin jacket. "Those are your words, sweet pea, not mine," he pointed out softly.

"But you're thinking them," she cried, "and you have no right. You don't know the half of what I went through after you disappeared off the face of the earth."

"No, I don't," he said, "any more than you know what actually happened to me. One of the reasons I'm here now is that I think we're both entitled to some enlightenment. But let's strike a deal: I won't ask your forgiveness for my sins of omission, if you won't ask mine for yours of commission."

"I don't need your forgiveness because I haven't done a damned thing wrong," she shot back, an anger she'd almost forgotten sparking in response to his. Wasn't this how it had always been between them? Raging passion, or raging fury? Sudden disagreements that erupted into flaming rows, followed by reconciliations whose intensity left them both drained and exhausted?

She sank into the chair behind her desk, the fight seeping out of her. "You know, we never would have made a go of marriage," she said wearily. "We're too much alike, both strong-willed—"

"*I*'m strong-willed," Adam contradicted. "*You*'re just willful. Your trouble is, you were indulged as a child and grew up believing you had a right to whatever your little heart desired. It probably made perfect sense that, when you realized you'd made a mistake in dismissing one potential marriage candidate, you should simply turn around and snag the first available man to take his place."

"Is that your explanation of why you were so quick to accept the decision to end our engagement?" she countered. "To avoid being chained to such a spoiled brat for the rest of your life?"

"Hardly!" He pushed himself away from the glass cabinet and she thought, as he crossed over to sit in a chair facing hers, that he limped a little. "If I'd wanted out of our engagement, I'd have said so up-front. Your family might have programmed you to believe it was your social duty to stop tongues wagging all over town by marrying the man you were sleeping with, but they never carried that much clout with me.''

Privately, Georgia felt her family ran a poor second to his grandmother when it came to trying to manipulate other people's lives but she wasn't about to get side-tracked by the issue now. She was, however, forced to accept the truth of the rest of his statement. Whatever else his faults, Adam Cabot had never been a coward.

''Why don't you stop trying to outdo yourself in insults and tell me what happened to you?'' she said. ''Where did you disappear to for so long, and why have you shown up now, when it's too late for either of us to go back and change things?''

''To answer your last question first, because—silly me!—I thought you might be pleased to discover I'm alive. And because I thought you deserved to hear the news from me before it became common knowledge all over town. As for the rest, official reports to the contrary, I didn't go down with my aircraft. I managed to eject and bail out, got swept miles off course by a howling blizzard, and ended up breaking a number of bones and doing various other bodily damage when I landed in the frozen wastes of the sub-Arctic. That I didn't get eaten alive by polar bears or die from exposure is entirely due to the kindly intercession of a band of nomadic Inuit hunters who, for reasons that escape me, find traipsing over the Polar Ice Cap a stimulating winter pastime.''

He made it sound so uttery reasonable and ordinary that she knew he was leaving out a good deal more than he was telling. ''That might have kept you away for a few weeks, Adam, but it hardly explains your being gone fifteen months.''

He shrugged. "Some things take time," he said ambiguously. "And considering the way we parted, you can't blame me for not being in too much of a hurry to get back to you."

Any sympathy she might have felt for him evaporated at that. "You're the one who put our future together in jeopardy and allowed your ego to lure you out of retirement for one last chance at flying glory."

"And you're the one who threw my ring in my face and told me to take a hike. 'Fly off the edge of the earth, for all I care,' you said. Well, I did the next second-best thing, sweet pea."

"You know I didn't really mean that!" Georgia's voice faltered for a moment as other memories of that last time together came surging back, but she'd be damned if she'd let them overwhelm her. She'd done all the crying she was going to do over this particular tragedy. "In case you've forgotten, Adam, we both said harsh things to each other. I called you selfish and chauvinistic and a lot of other things I'm ashamed to recall."

"And I accused you of being cold and ambitious, which was equally unkind and untrue. It was your independence, the fact that you were as much a rebel as I was, that first attracted me to you."

His voice was grave and sincere enough to soften granite. If she let him, he'd throw her life into turmoil a second time and hurt innocent bystanders in the process. Under cover of the desk, she dug her finger nails into the palms of her hands and plowed through the rest of what she had to say. "I'm not a rebel anymore, Adam. Ten days after you left, a uniformed stranger showed up at my door and told me that pieces of your precious fighter jet had been found scattered over miles but that there was no sign and absolutely no chance that you had survived. In the space of five minutes my world collapsed and nothing has been the same since, especially not me."

"I agree. The Georgia I used to know would never have made such a remarkable recovery from grief that she'd be ready to marry someone else so soon."

"Recovery?" Her voice cracked with emotion and she felt the tears pricking behind her eyes despite her most stringent effort to keep them in check. "I fell apart almost literally! I didn't sleep for weeks, didn't want to eat or go out of the apartment. I wished I had died with you, Adam, because I'd lost everything that truly mattered to me."

*More, in fact, than you can begin to guess!*

She squeezed her eyes shut, even though doing so meant the tears escaped and drizzled down her face. "I felt guilty. And angry. And alone."

"You don't know the first thing about being alone. You had your family."

"Who were no help at all. My mother could scarcely contain her relief at being spared having you for a son-in-law." Georgia swiped at the tears with the back of her hand, angry and appalled at the ease with which the misery was finding chinks in her armor.

Adam leaned over, plucked a tissue from the box on the corner of her desk, and passed it to her. "But your father must have cared. He was never mean-spirited like that."

"He was sympathetic but..."

"Too henpecked to dare take a stand." Adam nodded. "Yeah, I'd forgotten how thoroughly your mother and sister keep poor old Arthur in line."

"Precisely." She drew in a deep breath and managed to get herself under control again. "And that's when I found out what a real friend Steven was."

"Well, good old Steven," Adam jeered softly.

"He saved my life," Georgia shot back, declining to mention that it was thanks to Steven that she hadn't hemorrhaged to death when she'd miscarried Adam's baby in the kitchen of her apartment. "If it hadn't been for him, I don't know how I would have gone on. I felt responsible for what had happened to you."

"Rubbish!" Adam scoffed. "The prototype's malfunction had nothing at all to do with you."

"But I didn't know that. I nursed the idea that you'd been too preoccupied over our disagreement to pay proper attention to what you were doing. The guilt festered, made more complicated by the reaction of everyone I met. Pity is a corrosive thing when it's flung in your face every time you turn around. Steven saved my sanity."

"So what are you telling me?" Adam wanted to know. "That you're marrying him out of gratitude? That it's no great love affair?"

They were the same questions that had kept her awake most of last night. "It's not quite that simple," she wailed.

"It is to me," Adam said bluntly. "When a man finds himself staring death in the face, things become very simple. It's a case of fight or go under. So do you love Steven, or don't you?"

"Of course I love him!"

"Well, that's one of the things I came back to find out. Now that I know, I guess you and I have nothing more to say to each other." He rose and zipped up his jacket. "Have a happy life, Georgia," he said, and turned away.

Eyes suddenly swimming again, she watched as he covered the distance to the front doors. Sometimes, it seemed that was what she remembered most vividly of all their times together: her watching as he walked away from her. And every time, it broke her heart all over again.

*Let him go*! the voice of sanity begged. *Do it just one more time and you'll never have to do it again.*

Yes, she thought.

And promptly accused, in a woebegone little voice, "That's what you did after we broke up, too. Just turned and walked away without even kissing me goodbye."

# CHAPTER TWO

HE STOPPED and turned back to face her. He looked at her long and thoughtfuly then, as he retraced his steps, said with ominous intent, "Did I really? Well, that's one mistake I certainly don't have to repeat."

Georgia's heart flapped around behind her ribs like a chicken trying to save its neck from the hatchet but Adam didn't care. He just kept moving until he loomed no more than twelve inches from where she stood rooted to the plush blue carpet under her feet.

Trapped by the desk behind her and the reckless words she'd flung at him, she did the only thing she could without losing what was left of her pride. She tilted her head to one side and with regal condescension, offered him her cheek.

"Oh, no," he murmured, capturing her face in cool fingers and turning it back toward him and bending his head to hers. "Not like that at all. Like this."

As soon as he touched her, she fell apart. A soft roaring filled her mind, dimming her hearing and clouding her vision. Her legs buckled, sending her reeling into him for support. She grabbed at him blindly, intending only to anchor herself upright, and instead found herself smoothing her hands over his face in tactile renewal of its beauty.

His mouth lowered. She felt the warm drift of his breath against her lips. And then, in excruciating slow motion, he kissed her.

It wasn't aggressive, as kisses between a man and a woman often were. There was no audacity, no thrusting invasion of privacy. He simply settled his lips on hers and let them rest there. Yet, for all that, it was a lover's kiss, delicately, temptingly erotic. A hothouse flower on the brink of bursting into fragrant bloom—or more accurately, an echo so painfully sweet of a splendor she'd once known that she couldn't bear to let it end.

She pressed herself to him, winding her arms around his neck and softening her mouth in acquiescence. A murmur escaped her—a plea for just a little more, just a little longer—soft enough that only he could hear it, yet able to deafen completely all those parts of her brain that were trying so hard to scream out a warning.

The hopeless, helpless longings she'd stored away, having found a crack through which to escape, took full advantage but she was too enthralled to notice. All she cared about was that Adam responded to her overtures by sliding his arms tightly around her and directing the seductive finesse he'd always employed so well to a different turn, one no longer defined by propriety.

His mouth grew bold, investigative, cajoling. As if she weren't willing enough to surrender to its assault! He tested her lips, tasted them and, when they opened to him, accepted the implicit surrender they offered.

At least, she thought he did. Was so convinced, in fact, that it took a while for her to comprehend that he was declining after all. Not that he was so ungallant as to shove her away and remind her that she was supposed to be engaged to another man. He merely ended things. Slowly, regretfully even, but quite firmly, leaving her no choice but to abide by his refusal.

"Will that suffice?" he asked.

She wrapped her arms around her waist as the cool aftermath of his rejection infiltrated every pore of her skin to lay an icy wreath around her heart. Drawing in

a great shuddering breath, she managed to nod. "Yes,"
she said.

He prepared to leave again and had one foot out the
door before he tossed a final word over his shoulder.
"Liar," he said.

Adam strode across the sidewalk and out into the rain-
slick road, narrowly missing being hit by a van that
turned the corner too quickly. He barely noticed. It
wasn't his time to die; he'd already proved that with the
business up north a year ago. And he had weightier things
on his mind right now, like the lingering feel of Georgia
in his arms, and the fact that some parts of him hadn't
been the least bit impaired by crash-landing in the frozen
tundra of the Arctic.

"Hah," he muttered with fake insouciance to the
bronze statue of Eugene Piper that presided over the little
public garden in the middle of the square, "that'll teach
her!"

But it had taught him, too—a lesson he'd briefly been
disposed to forget: she was about to marry another man.
While he'd been recovering from multiple fractures of
the thigh, a dislocated shoulder and four broken ribs,
not to mention a coma brought on by trauma to the
brain and major bruising of just about every internal
organ he owned, she'd been casting her net at Steven
Drake.

The woman to whom he'd given his heart and his ring,
and for whom he'd been willing to give up a career that
he'd truly loved, had taken his apparent death in stride
and gone ahead with her life without missing a beat. So
what did he think he was doing, getting himself all fired
up over a kiss when he ought to be congratulating himself
on his lucky escape?

"Not that I expected her to spend the rest of her life alone, draped in widow's weeds and burning a candle under my photo, you understand," he grumbled to Eugene. "But couldn't she have waited a decent interval? And chosen to look a bit further afield than my best friend?"

Eugene stared sightlessly ahead, rain dripping off his face mournfully. *Some best friend, Adam, old buddy*!

"I don't blame him," Adam said defensively. "He's a nice guy who didn't see what was headed his way until it was too late to duck. And at least he didn't sweep me under the carpet the way she did. He showed some sort of conscience about the whole affair."

In fact, from what Beverley had said, Steven had done a lot more than that. During the weeks immediately following the jet's disastrous test flight, he'd been a frequent visitor at her house. He'd taken time out from consoling the bereaved fiancée to offer comfort to an opinionated, autocratic old lady who didn't have another soul in the world who really gave a damn about her once her grandson had apparently shuffled off.

"He actually asked my permission to court that foolish child," Beverley had told Adam, stemming her pleasure in his survival long enough to allude to Georgia with the customary disdain she reserved for all the Chamberlaines. "Under the circumstances I gave him my blessing and wished him luck. Heaven knows he's going to need it, marrying into that straitlaced lot."

She'd been referring, of course, to the long-standing feud between the Walshes and the Chamberlaines, two of Piper Landing's founding families. It went back two generations, to the time when his maternal grandfather, Simon, had dumped Georgia's paternal grandmother, Celeste, to marry Beverley. Well, the tables had been turned now, with a vengeance!

"In the long run it's probably just as well that things fell apart between Georgia and me," Adam confided to Eugene. "Hell, there's enough grief in the world without a man finding himself caught in the crossfire between warring in-laws, wouldn't you say?"

Although Eugene continued to stare commiseratingly into space, a young woman pushing a baby carriage through the little park heard Adam muttering to himself, flung him a startled glance, and gave him a wide berth.

Just then, the Courthouse clock struck the quarter hour, reminding him that he was taking Beverley to lunch at one. "Well, enough of this rubbish," he decided, turning up the collar of his jacket and heading for his grandmother's 1979 Rolls-Royce which he'd prudently parked on the far side of the square, just in case Georgia had spotted it and decided not to answer the door to her chichi little establishment. "All I need is to have it rumored abroad that I've come back from the dead with half my marbles missing and was spotted wandering around town talking to myself!"

The minute they were seated at their usual window table at the Riverside Club, Natalie Chamberlaine went into a recital of the prenuptial affairs being hosted during the coming week in Georgia's honor. What she forgot to mention, Samantha, Georgia's younger sister, supplied.

Georgia bent her mouth into what she hoped passed for a smile and tried to look interested. Apparently, she didn't try hard enough.

"You know, Georgia," her mother commented, visibly annoyed, "people are going to quite a lot of trouble for you. It seems to me that the least you could do is show a little enthusiasm and appreciation in return. It is the second time they've done this, after all."

"Yes." Samantha nodded smugly, secure in the knowledge that, unlike her older sister, she'd managed to get married on the first try without making a botch of things. "Smarten up, Georgia. It's not as if we're just recycling leftovers from the first time."

*Except for Adam*! Georgia thought, and fought to stifle a burst of hysterical laughter.

"Are you sure there's nothing wrong, dear?" Her mother peered at her narrowly. "You really don't seem yourself today."

Georgia toyed with her spinach salad. All morning long she'd debated on when and how to tell her family the news that was doing a great job of turning her nicely ordered world upside-down. But she'd held back because she knew there'd be an uproar from both her mother and sister when they heard. On the other hand, Adam wasn't exactly sneaking around in secret, so how long could she afford to wait before letting them in on the fact that he'd turned up again?

Perhaps now was as good a time as any, after all. If nothing else, it would keep the outcry of protests down to a dull roar because nothing less than seeing her daughters held up at gunpoint would allow Natalie Chamberlaine to indulge in public hysteria. It wasn't considered seemly behaviour for members of the upper echelon of Piper Landing society.

"Actually, there is something I need to tell you," Georgia admitted.

"I don't like your tone of voice," Natalie broke in, playing nervously with the string of pearls around her throat. "I don't like it at all, Georgia. It's not bad news, is it?"

"That all depends on your point of view, I suppose..."

"Oh, for God's sake, Georgia!" Samantha leaned back in her chair and rolled her eyes, very much the smart young matron thoroughly in charge of her own affairs and unable to comprehend why everyone else couldn't follow her fine example. "Are you going to spit it out, whatever it is, or would you like us to drag it out of you, one syllable at a time?"

When they had been children, Georgia had sometimes found Samantha so intolerable that she'd forgotten she was always supposed to act like a little lady and had hauled off and smacked her sister. She felt like doing the same thing now.

"I'm trying to find the words to lead up to this gently, Samantha," she said. "It's not something I feel I can just 'spit out'."

Doing her best to ignore Samantha's heaving sigh of exasperation, she glanced around the dining room, searching for the inspiration that would enable her to detonate her little bombshell casually and discreetly, with a minimum of aftershock. However, when her gaze fastened on the sight of Adam and his grandmother entering the dining room and being shown to a table not ten feet away, all thought of nonchalance or restraint fled her mind. "Adam isn't dead," she blurted out.

Natalie's head shot up, though not quite as high as her voice. "*What did you say*?"

"Adam isn't dead, Mother. I saw him last night, and again this morning."

"Georgia, if this is your idea of a joke..." Natalie groped for her wineglass.

But Samantha, too, had seen, and was staring fixedly across the room. "She isn't joking, Mother," she confirmed faintly.

Natalie swiveled round in her chair, her gasp of dismay attesting to what most of the other people in the room also were noticing: the not-so-late Lieutenant Colonel

Adam Cabot, large as life, sitting across from his grandmother and inspecting the menu.

Gradually becoming aware that the dining room had grown unusually silent, he looked around and found himself the object of everyone's stunned attention, not the least among them Natalie and Samantha. Excusing himself to his grandmother, he rose from the table. Georgia supposed it was too much to hope he wouldn't come over to theirs, and she was right.

"Hello, Mrs. Chamberlaine," he said, as easily as if he'd last seen her only the week before. "How are you?"

If there was one thing a person could depend on, Georgia thought, watching the exchange with horrified fascination, it was that Natalie Chamberlaine never forgot her manners. She rose beautifully, if shakily, to the occasion. "Very well, thank you, Adam. And you?"

"Never better," he said, all charming smiles.

Samantha didn't fare quite as well as her mother. "We thought you were dead," she said.

Adam's smile assumed an edge that would have cut glass. "Lovely to see you again, too, Sammie."

"People don't call me by that name now that I'm married," she said, smoothing her impeccably cut hair.

"Married? Little Sammie?"

Only Samantha could have missed the amused irony in his tone. "Yes," she said, and held out her hand defiantly to show off her broad platinum wedding ring.

Adam inspected it with the tolerant awe of an uncle admiring his niece's latest toy. "Very nice, Sammie."

Flushed with annoyance at his continued lack of proper respect, Samantha unwisely attempted to punish him. "In case you haven't heard, Georgia will be wearing one, too, next month at this time."

His smoky blue gaze switched then and settled gravely on Georgia. His smile faded. "Will she?" he said softly. "Are you sure?"

If his first question was directed at her sister, his second was meant exclusively for her. Georgia knew Adam too well to be mistaken about that.

She tried to look away but he held her prisoner in his gaze and refused to let go. To her horror, she felt herself being drawn into those sultry blue depths and suffused with another bout of unspeakable longing.

"Very sure," she croaked, her mouth so dry she could scarcely get the words out. But when she tried to relieve the situation by taking a sip of wine, her hand shook so badly that she had to set the glass down again in a hurry.

*No, you're not*, his eyes said. *You're remembering how it felt when I kissed you this morning and you're no longer sure of anything*.

"Why are you here?" Samantha asked belligerently.

"To have lunch with my grandmother. Does that offend you?" Adam answered, never once allowing his gaze to stray from Georgia.

"Of course not, Adam. That wasn't what Samantha meant at all. You can understand, I'm sure, that we're...well, 'taken aback' scarcely describes it." Fully in control of herself again, Natalie flicked her serviette much as a matador might have tried to deflect the attention of a wayward bull. "I'm sure you have a quite remarkable explanation for your absence and we'd love to hear it, but this is not the time. Your grandmother is obviously anxious to have you rejoin her. Please don't keep her waiting on our account."

"Oh, she's waited fifteen months for the pleasure of my company at lunch," Adam said, ignoring the hint and keeping his gaze glued to Georgia. "I think she can wait a couple of minutes more, or as long as it takes for me to offer my congratulations to the bride and her family."

"Listen, Adam!" Samantha, who never had learned when to leave well enough alone, wagged a finger at him. "We don't know where you've been for the last year or more and we don't particularly care, but one thing we do want to make clear: we won't stand for your causing trouble for the Chamberlaines again and disrupting another wedding. You're not going to make us the laughingstock of this town a second time."

"Were people laughing the last time?" he inquired mischievously. "How very unkind, considering that everyone thought I'd died a hero's death."

Samantha puffed up with righteous indignation. "Stop twisting my words. No one wished you dead in the first place and no one does now—as long as you don't try to disrupt Georgia's plans. But she's finally making the *right* marriage and we won't put up with your trying to spoil things for her."

Adam lifted his shoulders in a puzzled shrug. "Why are you so worried?" he said smoothly, his gaze continuing to burn into Georgia's soul. "If, as you claim to believe, everything's perfect, nobody *can* spoil things. But if there are hidden flaws..." He smiled and dropped his glance to Georgia's mouth, then down her throat to where her heart was fluttering madly beneath her silk blouse. "...well then, I'm afraid they'll surface sooner or later, no matter how hard you try to ignore them. Have a nice lunch, ladies."

"I never did like him," Samantha declared, stating the painfully obvious as he wove a path back to where Beverley Walsh waited for him. But her sister was in a minority, Georgia decided, watching as his progress was hampered by a number of other diners eager to express pleasure in his return from the dead.

Natalie, however, had other things on her mind than taking a poll of Adam's enduring popularity. "Georgia," she said urgently, her pretty brown eyes full of anxiety, "you're not having second thoughts about Steven, are you?"

"No," Georgia said, feeling as if an intolerable weight were compressing her chest.

"Are you sure, dear?"

"Yes," she said, because she wanted it so badly to be true. But the sad fact was, she couldn't tear her gaze away from Adam Cabot flirting merrily with the waitress who'd come to take his order, and the sight sliced like a blade through Georgia's heart. What had happened to those invisible lines of defense that had served her so well in recent months? Why had they fallen apart now, when she needed them most?

"Because you know, dear, everything's in place for the wedding," her mother went on. "The flowers, the caterers, the church—"

"Not to mention all the loot," Samantha cut in. "You don't want to go through that routine again, do you, Georgia, having to return all the gifts and write those tedious little notes of explanation and stuff. Remember how embarrassing that was?"

"Yes," Georgia said, clenching her hands under cover of the table to prevent herself from racing over and yanking out that brassy blond waitress's hair by the fistful. Wouldn't *that* set Piper Landing on its ear!

Completely out of patience with her daughter's in-attention, Natalie gathered up her purse, gloves and daughters. "Girls, I think we should get out of here before another disaster occurs."

"I agree," Samantha said, her first sensible comment of the day, as far as Georgia was concerned. "For God's sake, Georgia, stop staring at him like that. You'll be drooling next."

They hustled her out of the club and into the car with a speed that verged on panic. "You drive, Samantha. I want to talk to your sister," Natalie ordered, handing over the keys to the Cadillac before climbing into the back seat with Georgia.

And talk she did, all the way back to the studio. Nonstop and frantically, pointing out all the things that Georgia already knew: that she'd got her life on track finally; that Steven was the most eligible bachelor in town and was completely devoted to her; that Adam Cabot had always been too much of a maverick to make good husband material and she was lucky—*blessed*, in fact—not to have ended up marrying him because it would have spelled disaster.

And somehow, Georgia wrapped herself in the remains of that fuzzy shroud of remoteness that had been her salvation in the past, and managed to nod and smile in all the right places. Did it so well, indeed, that when they dropped her off in the square outside her studio, she stood on the pavement and waved calmly until the car turned the corner.

Then she let herself into the studio, pulled the blind down over the window, turned out all but the security lights, and set the alarm system before letting herself out into the street again and locking the door. She wouldn't be designing any more custom jewelry that day, nor the next, either.

It took very little time for her to drive home and pack a few essentials. Steven arrived just as she took the last load out to her car.

"Well," he said, taking in the suitcase stowed neatly in the open trunk. "It seems I got here just in time."

"I was going to stop by the bank and leave a note," she said.

"*Note*, Georgia?" The gentle reproof in his tone made her feel very, very small and unworthy. "Don't you think I deserve better than that?"

"You know what's happened, don't you?" she said miserably. "I wondered when you'd find out."

"Everybody knows," he said. "The whole town's buzzing."

"I imagine he'll be in touch with you before the day's over."

Steven eyed the suitcase again. "I gather he's already been in touch with you and that's why you're running away."

"I'm not running away," she insisted. "I'm in a state of shock and I just need to spend a little time alone to sort through a few things." She made a helpless gesture with her hand. "I can't do that here, Steven, so I thought I'd go up to your family's chalet. Between commissions at work and a social calendar that's fully booked from now until the wedding day, I won't have a minute to myself and...."

He watched her, his honest gray eyes full of compassion. "Are we still going to have a wedding day, Georgia?" he asked, when at last she dribbled into silence.

He was a good man, a fine man. He was her best friend. If she married him, she would never know a moment's insecurity or want. He would love her, cherish her, and gladly forsake all others for her. At the very least, he deserved her honesty now. "I don't know," she said.

He nodded sadly. "Then you must go and find out. Take your time, love. I'll cover for you here."

The fine thread by which she'd been hanging on to her control snapped at that. Like a child, she covered her face with her hands and burst out crying.

He reached out and held her, sheltering her in his arms, and she wished with all her heart that she could stay there and not have to face tomorrow. "I hate him," she sobbed. "I don't want things to be spoiled like this, and it's all his fault."

Steven stroked her hair. "It's nobody's fault, Georgia."

"But I was so sure about us, until he showed up again."

"I know." He pulled away a little and just for a moment his resolution wavered enough to let his own pain show. "Georgia, marry me tonight. Let's just go away and leave all this behind. So what if Adam has come back? You and I have been happy together, haven't we? We can be again."

Temptation lured, promising the easy road. But for how long? She shook her head. "I can't," she whispered.

He sighed heavily and slackened his hold. "No, I suppose not."

She pulled away and accepted the handkerchief he offered. "Will your parents mind my using the chalet?"

"Of course they won't. But will you be all right by yourself? There's already been snow in the mountains and more is expected. The road might be bad."

"I know. I'll be careful."

He held open the driver's door of her car. "Then you'd better get going."

She had never loved him more. Heavy with the knowledge that she was playing fast and loose with a man who was a prince by any standards, she backed down the driveway and drove to the outskirts of town, stopping only at the supermarket where she stocked up on enough groceries to get her through the next few days, and again at the service station to fill up with gas.

Daylight was just beginning to fade as she left Piper Landing and took the highway north toward the mountains.

Adam went for a long walk along the far side of the river that afternoon, partly as therapy to help restore the muscle tone in his injured leg and partly to get away from the general curiosity that his reappearance was arousing.

He supposed it was natural enough that people were interested, but what they didn't seem able to appreciate was that he felt a bit like a goldfish in a bowl. And it was a difficult adjustment for a man who'd spent over a year in an isolated hunting camp in the Arctic.

What had really rattled him, though, had been running into the Chamberlaine women at lunch, with half Piper Landing society witness to the confrontation. He thought he'd acquitted himself well enough in the verbal exchange, but when he'd happened to glance up halfway through his meal to see Georgia being whisked away, he'd been unable to stop himself from swiveling in his chair and gazing after her with the lovelorn fascination of some twerp in an old black and white melodrama.

The plain fact was, she'd changed, and he wanted to acquaint himself with the new woman. Where before she'd been sculpted angles from her short, smart haircut to her elegant suits, now she flowed in softly feminine lines. Her hair kissed her shoulders, swirling over the ruffled nonsense of her blouse collar.

Her coat, winter-white where once she'd have chosen red or black, flared almost to her ankles. Her boots, her sole concession to the late November weather, were suede, with little dainty heels and tassels. Dancer's footwear, delicate enough to perform a *pas de deux*.

But most of all, her eyes were different. Not in their color, that brilliant teal blue arresting enough to stop traffic, nor in their dramatic, heavily lashed shape borrowed from God knew which exotic ancestor, but in their intensity. The sharp, dissecting focus was gone, replaced by a muted dreaminess. Her gaze seemed to slide over the world, a hazy blue waterfall that didn't quite notice the objects in its path.

It disturbed him. More, it annoyed him. He wanted to shake her, shock her into awareness, before it was too late.

Too late for what? For them? Hell, there was no "them" anymore; hadn't been since she'd told him to forget marriage. And he really must be missing a few marbles to be freezing his butt in the cold, damp mist rising from the river, and rehashing something which he ought, by now, to have accepted.

His grandmother was intensely annoyed at being left to her own devices all afternoon and let him know it the minute he let himself in the house. "May one assume you intend to dine at home tonight, Adam?" she inquired frostily, appearing in the doorway to the library with her thick white hair skewered in a knot and held in place by a knitting needle on top of her head. "Or do you plan to abandon me for the evening, too?"

He grinned, his good humor restored by the roaring fire and the good, stiff Scotch she had waiting for him. "I thought I'd stick around and wipe the floor with you at cards since I don't have a better offer," he said, not the least bit perturbed by her sharp tongue.

She snorted and mumbled that absence hadn't done much for his manners, but once dinner was over and she was three hundred points up on him at two-handed bridge, she mellowed a little.

"Pour me another vodka," she ordered, and thought he didn't notice that she leaned over to sneak a look at his cards when his back was turned.

"You're the only eighty-one-year-old I know who downs vodka like water and who cheats at cards," he said, refilling her glass.

"Don't be a sore loser, boy," she said, delving into the box of Russian Sobranis at her side and lighting up the one cigarette she allowed herself every evening. "It's the mark of poor upbringing."

The doorbell spared him the necessity of having to field an answer to that observation. "Expecting company, Bev?"

"No," she said. "Get rid of them, whoever they are."

But that was easier said than done. When Adam opened the door, the man who knew him better than almost anyone else on earth waited on the other side. "Hi," Steven said. "I heard you were back."

"Yeah," Adam said, an unsettling mix of pleasure and rage taking hold of him at the sight of his one-time best friend. "I should have called you."

"Why haven't you?"

Adam threw him a level look. "You know why."

"Yes. And I think it's time we talked about it."

His grandmother's imperious tone floated out from the library. "Who is it, Adam?"

"Steven," he said, then added to the man still standing on the front porch, "You'd better come in. This might take some time."

Beverley greeted the visitor with a marked lack of conviviality. "Why aren't you out celebrating with all your male friends and cheering raucously as some half-naked female jumps out of a cake, Steven Drake, since

I know for a fact that you're getting married very shortly?"

"Because I don't know that for a fact," Steven said. "And that's the reason I'm here now."

"Why? It's none of our business how you choose to ruin your life."

Steven's gaze swung from Bev to Adam and remained there. "I'm not sure Adam and I agree with you, Mrs. Walsh."

They had met when they'd been assigned as roommates in their first semester of boarding school. It had been one of those tough establishments whose Latin motto loosely translated into: WE MAKE MEN OF THEM IF WE DON'T KILL THEM FIRST.

In that sort of environment, a kid of thirteen needed an ally he could trust. Adam and Steven had liked each other on sight and long ago had perfected the sort of telepathic communication that exists between true friends. There was no need for Steven to elaborate on his statement now.

That didn't stop Beverley, however. "I hope you're not accusing Adam of—" she began, tottering to her feet.

"Shut up, Beverley," Adam said, and when she prepared to protest such uncavalier treatment, said again, "Sit down and shut up. This is between me and Steven."

"Is it?" Steven asked levelly, cutting to the heart of the matter. "Or is it still between you and Georgia?"

# CHAPTER THREE

FIFTEEN miles from where the private lane to the Drake chalet branched off from the main highway, it started to snow, dense fat flakes that cut visibility in half and added quickly to the foot or more that had fallen during the previous week.

Cranking up the car heater as high as it would go, Georgia huddled over the steering wheel, stepped gently on the accelerator, and prayed she wouldn't come to grief on the last long incline that led to the cabin. If the car got stuck, she'd have no choice but to climb out into the teeth of the blizzard and try to fit her tires with the chains she kept in the trunk in case of emergency.

The problem was, she was far from certain she knew how to go about the task since such an emergency had never before arisen. And crouching on a mountainous back road, in the dark, in the middle of a snowstorm, didn't strike her as a propitious place to find out.

As it happened, she had nothing to worry about. Someone had taken a blower and cleared a swath wide enough to enable her to drive right up to the property and park in the lee of the chalet's wide, overhanging balcony.

The same someone had turned on the electric generator and split enough wood to heat a church. In the big main room, a pyramid of kindling lay waiting in the fireplace, with a basket of seasoned alder logs close by. A lamp burned on a side table, next to a thermos of coffee.

Although her down-filled coat shielded her from the worst of the weather, by the time Georgia had unloaded her supplies and hauled them inside, her hands and feet were numb with cold. Before stowing everything away, she set a match to the kindling and poured herself a mug of the coffee.

She was only partially thawed when footsteps clumped up the steps and a fist banged on the door. It was Arne Jensen, the Drakes's nearest neighbor and the only year-round resident of the area. A tall, spare man in his late fifties who lived alone and socialized little, his sole concession to modern amenities was the telephone he'd had installed in his A-Frame cabin three winters before.

"Oh, *ja*, you got here then," he declared, his singsong Scandinavian accent as pronounced as the day he'd first come to North America. "I wanted to make sure."

Georgia smiled for what seemed like the first time in days. "I might have known you're the one I have to thank for all this, Arne. How did you know to expect me?"

"Mr. Drake, he phoned late this afternoon. Wanted me to check up and see that you had everything you need."

"That was thoughtful of him, and I do, thanks."

"Good. Then I will go. The weather is getting worse. We're in for a very big storm tonight."

He was right. In the last half hour, the wind had risen to a mournful howl, a fitting accompaniment for Georgia's mood. How could she jeopardize her future with Steven like this, she wondered, closing the door on Arne. What perverse streak of madness had brought her up here, away from a man who loved her enough to make sure she was safe and comfortable, even when she was running away from him?

Except it wasn't Steven she was trying to escape, it was Adam, and she'd run about as far as she could go. It was time to stop, face the memories he resurrected, and exorcise them forever.

The fire had taken hold and was throwing out a decent heat, enough to make the room cozy. If it wasn't quite enough to thaw the chill inside her, the liberal dash of brandy with which she spiked her coffee promised to do the trick.

This far from town, radio reception was nonexistent but there was a stereo with a CD player on a shelf next to the fireplace. She selected five discs at random and set the volume to low. Linda Ronstadt filled the room with soulful nostalgia, crooning a lament for love gone wrong.

Until today, the chalet had always been special with its wide-planked wooden floors covered with woven rugs, its pine-paneled walls, its great floor-to-ceiling stone fireplace. A happy place, where Steven had proposed, how could it now seem so spoiled?

Deciding she had neither the energy nor the appetite to prepare a meal, Georgia stored the groceries, added more wood to the fire and turned off the lights. And then, because there was nothing else she could do to put off the inevitable, she climbed into the chair, pulled a lap quilt over her knees, and tried to figure out a way to banish the uncertainty that had beset her in the last twenty-four hours.

It was quite straightforward, really. All she had to do was accept that although Adam might not be dead, the love they'd shared was, erased by too many tears and the sweet, generous devotion of another man.

Once she came to terms with that, she could drive back to Piper Landing and pick up her future, the one she and Steven had planned together. The nice, conventional, predictable future that her family approved of. The kind any normal, healthy woman would give her right arm for.

She was past the first flush of youth, after all. And surely, at thirty-two, she knew better than to hang on to the sort of romantic ideals in which only the very young and naive believed. Didn't she?

*Even if it meant settling for second best?*

She closed her eyes, hoping that by doing so she could silence the tiny voice that clamored to be heard. Immediately, Adam swam into her mind's eye, his image startlingly clear.

"Steven's not second best," she whispered. "He's exactly what I want."

*Want?* the voice mocked. *You haven't known the meaning of the word "want" since you thought Adam had died.*

Well, so what if, this time, there wasn't the passion she'd known with Adam? How could she expect there would be when she and Steven had decided to wait until after marriage to make love? She'd never been the kind to leap easily into physical intimacy, and Steven was too much a gentleman to coerce her into abandoning the principles that had served her for most of her life.

Unlike Adam. She'd succumbed to *his* advances on their second date, tumbling shamelessly into the back seat of his grandmother's Rolls and discarding her twenty-seven-year-old virginity without a moment's regret. During the two weeks before he was due back at his station in Alaska, they'd made love again and again at more spots around town than Georgia cared to remember. Anywhere and everywhere; recklessly, feverishly, magnificently.

She'd have married him then if he'd asked her, but he hadn't. And she, the avowed career woman in the family, the one who'd publicly declared that she had no room in her life for marriage, had suddenly wanted it with a passion that verged on obsession.

To her dismay, she soon realized that she had a rival. Not another woman—even in her madness, she'd never have accepted that humiliation—but Adam's career. His love affair with her had been placed repeatedly on a back burner while he catered to his other mistress, flying. And it did everything it could to rob her of him, quite literally placing his life in danger every time he took to the skies.

They had begun to quarrel. The times when they could be together, that she anticipated so eagerly, ended more often than not in arguments. The times apart were even worse and she'd worry that perhaps their last disagreement had killed his love for her; that, this time, he wouldn't come back. But he always did, and the passion would flame anew, consuming them both.

"Let's not spoil things by getting married," he'd say. "What we've got is too good to fall victim to the rot that killed the spark between your folks—not that mine were any better."

He didn't often mention his parents. She knew that he'd been the only child of a U.S. military man and his Canadian wife, a couple who were absent so much that when they drowned in a boating accident off the coast of West Africa, their death caused barely a ripple in the life of the child who'd split his time between Beverley Walsh and boarding schools. "If I ever have kids, they'll never grow up the way I did," he'd once said. "They'll be able to count on their old man to be there when they need him."

Was that what had finally wrung a proposal from him? The need to feel part of a family? A jealousy of her career that almost matched her fear of his?

She'd never known, had simply accepted with prayerful gratitude his decision to retire from active service and settle into marriage. If, sometimes, he'd seemed unusually moody, she'd chosen not to look too closely for the cause. She'd thought the worst was over, that the diamond on her finger was a talisman that would ward off all evil and make the sacrifice seem worthwhile.

She'd learned differently the day the call came from his old Commanding Officer. She'd known then that she'd had to give him the chance of freedom, even though she could have told him about her pregnancy and clipped his wings forever.

In the background, Natalie Cole held the stage, bridging the chasm between life and death in poignant duet with a father she'd lost when she was still a child. *Unforgettable....*

The images in Georgia's mind blurred, one merging with another and assaulting her without mercy. Stueben crystal and Christian Dior china, and Adam gate-crashing the first bridal shower, his irreverence for tradition turning the sedate affair into a riotous party.

A wedding dress of white satin and French lace, chosen with care to complement the irresistible glamor of Adam in dress uniform. Tea roses and orchids, romantic and formal—and the sheer delight of finding her bed scattered with dozens of sweet peas, filched from somebody's garden, the night before she sent him away.

Her last tangible link with him, the baby neither of them had planned but which had been conceived anyway, broken when she miscarried three weeks later, the frail new life torn away by too much grief.

Life and laughter; death and tears.

And afterward, the silence. Vast and empty as the Arctic landscape that had taken him from her, it deserted her only for dreams so real that she'd wake with her senses full of him. His scent, his touch, the sound of his voice....

A swift flare of light arcing across the paneled walls snapped her back to the present. Its engine, muffled by the snow and overlaid by the wind outside and the music within, had prevented her from hearing the approach of the vehicle until it growled to a stop next to her car.

Trailing the lap quilt after her, she opened the door and waited. The newcomer was just a smudge in the gray opalescence of the snow-flocked night, but she knew him, would always know him, no matter how many years or tragedies kept them apart.

He climbed the steps, stamping snow from his boots, and strode past her into the cabin without a word. A layer of flakes clung to his hair; a few others slid off the shoulders of his leather jacket. He looked tired, the limp she'd thought she detected that morning more pronounced. It lent a severity to his mouth, bracketing it with narrow grooves of tension, but his eyes were as blue and unflinching as ever.

She was not surprised to see him. She'd known it was he from the moment his headlights had flashed a warning through the room.

His arrival stripped her clean, leaving her neither happy nor sad, fearful nor angry. Instead, she felt removed from herself, a spectator of human folly about to witness a mighty battle to end, once and for all, a war that had started three autumns before.

Her mistake, she recognized disinterestedly, had not been in coming up here to resolve the issues. It had been in thinking she could do so alone. An arena containing only one adversary was nothing more than a vacuum.

"Was the road bad?" she asked, closing the door and going to the fire to add more wood.

"Yes." His voice emerged muffled and she glanced over her shoulder to find him toweling the melting snowflakes from his hair.

"There's coffee in the thermos over there, or brandy if you prefer it."

"Is that how you've been passing the time?" Throwing the towel over the back of a chair, he picked up her mug and sniffed the cold contents suspiciously. "Sitting here getting plastered to numb you to the reality of what you've done?"

No need to ask what he meant by that. The first shot had been fired and there would be no backing off now until one of them surrendered. "All I have done is try to put the fabric of my life back together," she said.

"And torn apart two others to do it."

"Two?"

He nodded, supremely confident that he had all the answers. "Steven came to see me earlier. We've known each other for twenty-five years. He's the closest thing to a brother I've ever had. From the time we were teenagers until our careers made other demands on us, we shared every birthday, every Christmas. He has remained my best friend through good times and bad. Until tonight when, because of you, we were barely able to speak half a dozen words to each other."

She recognized the edge in his voice that warned there was fire beneath his icy calm but she wouldn't—couldn't—allow it to penetrate the apathy that was now so much a part of her. "Really?"

"Does that please your vanity, Georgia?" he asked.

"No," she said calmly, "it does not. I am not a prize to be awarded to the winner in some neolithic male ritual. And if anyone's vanity is involved here, Adam, it's yours. I did not agree to become Steven's wife to punish you, or to make me forget you. I agreed because of all the fine and enduring qualities that make him the man he is, and because I thought we could have a good and satisfying life together."

"Keep this up long enough," Adam sneered, "and you might convince yourself, but don't expect me to buy it for a minute."

"You don't enter into it," she said, experiencing the mild satisfaction of knowing that she'd scored a hit without leaving herself open to further attack from him. "I'm afraid you played no part at all in my decision because you were part of the past and if there is one thing I'm sure of it's that, no matter how badly we might wish otherwise, there is no going back to what used to be."

"You're a liar," he said flatly. "Ever since I reappeared, you've been so mired in the past you're barely able to function. And the only thing you're sure about is that it's not over between you and me, and it never will be. What you can't decide is if your dishonesty extends to allowing you to marry one man when you know you're lusting after another."

She'd known that, sooner or later, the fighting would get dirty. She just hadn't known exactly when and that it came so soon caught her off guard. But she also knew that her best refuge was to remain inside that now habitual cocoon of indifference, so she shrugged lightly and turned toward the kitchen. "You wish."

"I *know*," he said, following after her.

She edged around the circular pine table and four chairs which separated kitchen area from living room. "You don't know beans," she said recklessly, goaded by his certainty into forsaking caution. "Steven's too good a lover for me to be harboring sexual fantasies about you or any other man."

He prowled after her, his laughter making a mockery of her assertion. "Is that why you begged me to kiss you, this morning? And when I was gracious enough to comply, is that why you kissed me back with such devouring hunger?"

"You're letting your imagination run away with you."

"And you're telling lies again, Georgia."

On her way around the table, she pulled out one of the chairs in an effort to impede his stalking maneuvers. "You're as infuriating as ever, if not more so."

"And you're still as selfish," he said, casually stepping over the chair.

"You're arrogant. Conceited."

"With reason." He smirked.

"I'm glad I gave you back your ring."

"Good," he said, closing the gap between them. "So am I."

Oh, God! she thought numbly. They were doing it again. Resorting to cheap, nasty shots, just like before. Silly, juvenile taunts, meant to hurt. As though behaving like children would camouflage the deeper issues. As though dealing with each other honestly would bare more truths than either of them had the courage to face.

She pulled out another chair and almost tripped over it herself trying to escape him. "I don't know why I wasted a single tear on you," she fumed, any hope she had of maintaining a serene front shriveling in the heat of her exasperation. "I should have married Steven a lot sooner."

He pounced then, his anger outracing hers and running wild as a forest fire. Picking up the chair, he flung it aside so violently that one of the legs snapped as it crashed to the floor. "Then what are you doing, holing up here?" he snarled, reaching out and grabbing her wrist with unforgiving strength. "If you're so certain that's what you want, get your stuff and hit the road. I won't stand in your way."

"Take your hands off me!" she snapped, as he strong-armed her toward the door. "I'm not going anywhere on your say-so, especially not on a night like this. I'd be a fool."

His anger didn't so much fade as assume a different energy. The compressed line of his mouth softened, the blue of his eyes deepened to wood smoke, as his gaze fastened on her. "You'll be a bigger fool if you stay," he said hoarsely. "Wait until tomorrow and it'll be too late."

She glared at him, refusing to let him know the extent of the upheaval his threat stirred in her. "I'll take my chances," she said rashly, discretion definitely not evincing itself as the better part of valor.

Adam looked away first. "Suit yourself," he muttered, letting go of her and putting a safe distance between them.

What in God's name had he thought he could accomplish by following her up here? That sheer physical force would be enough to wrestle a confession from her? That belittling her motives and denigrating her feelings would convince her of the error of her thinking?

It had seemed plausible enough a few hours ago, and he knew that was precisely the reason Steven had volunteered her whereabouts. "She's caught between a rock and a hard place and she's running out of time," he'd said. "If you and I are ever going to be friends again, one of us is going to have to force the issue with her. Under the circumstances, I think it had better be you."

"Why me?" Adam had asked, all the while knowing he'd no intention of being the one left behind. "Why not you?"

"Because I'm not the loose cannon around here, you are, and we both know it," Steven had replied, shaming Adam with his candor.

And he had the nerve to call Georgia dishonest!

He picked up the brandy bottle and waved it in her general direction. "Do you want another shot of this?"

"Why not?" she replied, in that zombie fashion that she appeared to favor these days. He'd shake her loose from that before he'd done!

He found two glasses in the cupboard and pulled up another armchair before the fire. For a while, they said nothing to each other, merely nursed their drinks and private thoughts, and stared into the flames.

"What are you going to do?" he finally asked.

She bit her lip and downed the rest of her brandy in one gulp before she answered, "I'm going to marry Steven in two and a half weeks' time."

Adam hadn't ached quite so painfully since the early days of his recovery. "You really love him, huh?"

"Yes," she said. "We're good for each other."

He was a bloody fool to ask, but he did it anyway. "As much as you used to love me?"

"It's different," she said. "With you, it was all passion and rage and suffering. With Steven, there's a kindness, a fine balance that soothes and quiets the pain."

He grimaced. "Sounds like a headache remedy to me."

"Not quite," she replied piously. "More like something to ease the indigestion resulting from a meal that was always a little too..."

"Rich?" He arched one eyebrow derisively. "Are you telling me you prefer a blander diet?"

"Perhaps," she said, plastering a saintly, long-suffering expression on her face.

"Heavens, Georgia!" he exploded. "You used to be a real pistol! What happened to you?"

She turned her head away and didn't answer. He reached around and grasped her chin, forcing her to face him again. "Georgia?"

Her eyes were sparkling with tears. "I just want peaceful, easy loving, the sort you and I were never able to find. I don't have the energy to fight all the time."

It had never been her style to bow to defeat so easily. She'd always been the kind to fight back, a prime example of the old maxim that when the going got tough, the tough got going. "Why, Georgia," he murmured, "don't you know that settling for so little is sentencing you both to a lifetime of misery?"

"It won't be misery," she quavered, her mouth trembling. "I won't allow it to be. I'll make a career out of being happily married. That's what women had to do a hundred years ago and I can do it now."

He wanted to kiss that mouth but dared not, because things wouldn't stop there. A kiss had never been enough to stem the hunger where she was concerned.

Before temptation got the better of him, he took his hand away from her face and said, "Do you really think Steven won't know that it's all an act?"

"I'll make him happy enough that he'll never have reason to suspect," she said, with an intensity that hinged more on desperation than conviction. "And his happiness will rub off on to me so that, after a while, it won't be an act anymore. There'll be other children and we'll be a family, and then I'll be able to forget—"

She broke off suddenly, and clapped a hand to her mouth but he was too wrought up himself to question why. The thought of her conceiving a child that wasn't his was more than Adam could bear. He grabbed the bottle and splashed enough brandy into his glass to dull an elephant's misery. "All right, I get the picture!"

"Does that mean you'll go away and leave us alone?" she asked in a small, hopeful voice.

He wasn't going to make it that easy for her. "If, by that, you mean will I conveniently disappear off the face of the earth again, I'm afraid not. You're not the only one with obligations to someone else. My grandmother went through her own hell when she thought I'd died and I owe it to her to stick around for a while."

"But what about the Air Force? Don't you have to report back soon?"

"Only for a short time, just long enough to retire again, this time for good," he said wearily. "It took a while but I finally came to the realization that you were right, Georgia. I'm past my prime as a flying ace and it's time to hand over to the bright young sparks coming up behind me."

Her lovely aquamarine eyes scrutinized him. "I don't believe that," she said softly. "You're the best test pilot they ever had and that's why, when they ran into problems, they called on you to help them out. And you thrived on the danger."

"Then let's just say that, during the long months of my healing and convalescence, living to a ripe old age acquired an appeal it never had before. There's something about coming face to face with his own mortality, Georgia, that gives a man a new perspective on the value of life."

"But what will you do instead?"

He shrugged, unwilling to tell her that, in his present frame of mind, nothing held much attraction. "I'm looking at a number of options."

"In Piper Landing?"

"Perhaps." He held her gaze. "Does that bother you?"

"It shouldn't," she said miserably.

"But?"

"I think it would be better if we weren't always running into each other."

"Better for whom, Georgia?"

"For all of us." Her troubled gaze implored him. "Adam, please don't make this any harder than it already is."

"I'm not doing anything, sweet pea. You're the one choosing to run headlong into trouble."

She sighed and compressed her sweet mouth into that stubborn line he knew so well. "I can see that appealing to your better nature is a waste of time."

"Jeez, what do you want of me?" he snapped, the maelstrom of emotions she stirred in him suddenly boiling up anew. "I suffer months of agony but manage to hang on in the belief that when I get back, we'll both be older and wiser and our little spat will have blown over. But when I miraculously show up alive, you make no secret of the fact that I'd have done you a bigger favor by staying dead. Your mother and sister make me feel about as welcome as warts on a princess. Not once do any of you ask me what I've gone through, or how I managed to survive when all the odds say I shouldn't have. But do I snivel or make a scene? Do I threaten revenge or ill-wish you?" He glared at her. "Well, do I?"

"You haven't exactly—"

"The answer," he roared, "is, no, I don't. On the contrary, I'm being a bloody good sport, all things considered."

"A good sport," she replied self-righteously, "wouldn't try to make trouble by kissing me the way you did this morning."

"If I was interested in making trouble for you, sweet pea," he drawled, "we wouldn't be sitting here now arguing the point. We'd be stark naked and doing what we've always done so well together. And just to set the record straight, you're the one who got things started this morning, as well as the one who showed no inclination to call a halt when they showed signs of getting out of hand. Yet you have the goddamned nerve to accuse *me* of lacking a better nature.''

"This conversation is getting us nowhere,'' she said, a delicate flush running under her skin.

"You're right. We're going over the same old stuff and getting no further ahead, so why don't we just can it and get some sleep instead?'' He shoved himself to his feet and stretched, when what he really wanted was to punch his fist through the nearest wall. "Which do you prefer, the bed in the loft or the pull-out sofa down here?''

"I'll take the sofa.''

"Fine. I'll see you in the morning.''

"Not if I can avoid it. I plan to be out of here at first light.''

"Rushing back to your bridgegroom's arms?''

"Exactly. It's where I belong. The pity of it is that I didn't realize it sooner. I could have spared myself the ordeal of driving up here then, not to mention the greater tribulation of having to deal with you.''

Exactly what had triggered his fury he didn't know, nor had he expected it. It had come sneaking up and taken him as much by surprise as it had obviously taken her. Worse, it showed no sign of abating and he didn't like that. It left him too much at the mercy of his emotions; too liable to say things he'd live to regret.

It was a funny thing, he thought, shucking off all but his briefs and diving under the goose feather duvet on the old-fashioned sleigh bed in the loft. There'd been a time not so long ago when he'd have have bartered any amount of regret in exchange for the guarantee of remaining alive. But that was when he'd thought Georgia would be waiting for him and they could start over again.

The mattress had lumps in it and sagged in the middle. God, where had the Drakes acquired it, he wondered irritably, punching the pillows and trying to find a position that gave relief to his aching leg and back. And how the hell could it still be so cold up here when it was warm as toast down there where she was getting settled for the night?

He could hear the sound of her undressing, the unmistakable rustle of silky, secret underthings sliding over heat-flushed skin. And suddenly it wasn't the ache in his back or his leg that had him thrashing around. It was desire fueled by despair, and a host of kaleidoscopic images of how she used to look without clothes, all smooth, delicious female curves as warm and inviting as paradise itself.

"Son of a bitch!"

Flinging aside the pillows, he sat up and raked back the hair from his forehead. Reflection from the fire downstairs threw light across the cedar beams overhead, tempting him to lean over the half wall of the loft and sneak a look at her, but hell would freeze over before he'd give in to the urge.

Ramming the pillows behind his head, he tried again to settle himself for sleep. During the early days of his recovery, when it had hurt excruciatingly even to breathe, one of the Inuit men had taught him a sort of autohypnosis. He'd learned to focus his concentration so thoroughly on some external object that there was no room for the internal pain to gain ascendance.

He tried the same technique now. High on the opposite wall, a circular stained-glass window just below the apex of the roof glowed ruby in the subdued fire-light. He fixed it in an unblinking gaze, forced himself to breathe deeply and evenly, relaxed every taut muscle, and waited.

Without success.

From somewhere behind the head of the bed the wind found entry through a crevice and streamed inside the loft, a wicked icy trickle that crept down his neck to dilute the feeble warmth beneath the duvet.

Jeez, but it was cold! Colder than it had ever been in the Inuit camp and certainly cold enough to kill any lustful notions he might have harbored a half an hour earlier. He could use another shot of brandy to chase away the chill and numb his brain. Hell, he could use the whole damn bottle!

He raised his head and listened intently. Apart from the odd spit and crackle from the fire, it was quiet downstairs with the sort of deep and peaceful silence of a house at rest. At least *she* was able to sleep.

He inched out of bed, cringing a little as his bare feet hit the floor, stole to the head of the stairs and listened again. Nothing. At least, nothing from inside the cabin though the wind still howled outside.

He tried to be quiet. Just how well he succeeded became apparent when he reached the bottom stair and saw that Georgia wasn't asleep, after all. She wasn't even under the covers of the sofa bed. Instead, she sat crouched on the edge of the hearth, her head bowed and her long blond hair hanging forward to obscure her face.

He froze, unable to tear his gaze away. Appalled at what he saw. Terrified of what to do about it.

He knew she'd lost weight since he'd been gone but only now, seeing her in nothing but a nightgown, did he realize to what extent. She was elfin in her fragility, almost transparent. And she was crying with quiet, contained desperation. The sight slammed him in the solar plexus like an iron fist.

# CHAPTER FOUR

UNCERTAIN what to do, Adam hesitated and must have made some slight noise because she looked up and saw him hovering at the foot of the stairs. The firelight turned her tear tracks to strands of gold before she smeared them with the back of her hand.

"I thought you were in bed," she said.

"I was."

"So what are you doing spying on me?"

"I'm not. It's freezing up there and I came down to get something to warm me up."

"Oh, sure!" Saturated with tears, her scornful laughter floated across the room. "And you thought I'd do nicely for the job."

"Actually, I came to get that." He indicated the brandy bottle on the table next to the sofa. "And just for the record, it's not my style to move in on another man's woman when his back is turned."

His shot found its mark. Even in the semi-darkness, he saw the blush that flared across her cheeks before she turned her face away from him. "Then why did you follow me up here?"

"Because I thought my being here might help you to decide what it is you really want. Why were you crying?"

Wrapping her arms around her legs, she rested her head on her knees and he thought again how fragile she looked in a way that went beyond the comformation of bone and flesh. There was a dimming of the spirit about her, as if she'd turned off some vital inner light.

"Because I'm miserable and confused," she confessed, staring into the fire. "And frightened."

He wove a path around the sofa bed and picked up the brandy bottle. "The Georgia I once knew was never afraid of anything."

"I've changed."

"Yes," he said, "you have. The fight's gone out of you, Georgia. How come?"

"I've grown up."

"Is that what you call it?" Her hair shimmered pale gold about her shoulders. He couldn't help himself; he bent down and sifted a handful through his fingers. It felt warm and alive in the way that she used to be. "It strikes me as more like giving up. You're going through the motions of living, doing and saying all the things other people expect of you, but your heart's not in it, and though you might fool everyone else, you don't fool me. What killed the spark, Georgia?"

She flinched at his touch and almost said, "Grieving did it. I lost so much—you, your child—that I became one of the walking dead myself. Perfectly preserved on the outside, perfectly hollow within. And now you're back and I'm afraid to trust my heart to you again because you've changed, too. There's a wariness about you that's new. It's put distance between us and you're not willing to meet me halfway, and I cannot—*dare* not— bridge the gap alone."

But that called for more honesty than she dared deliver, so she skated around the full truth and settled for a half measure with a question of her own. "What would you do if I called off the wedding?"

"I'd respect your decision."

Dismay flooded through her. "Is that all?"

He picked up the brandy bottle and tilted it, first one way, then the other, so that the liquor flowed back and forth in an amber tide. "What else would you like me to do?"

"Well, would you...?" She stopped and ran her tongue over lips grown dry with apprehension. "...Would we...?"

He held the bottle very still between both his hands and looked at her. She tugged her nightgown tight around her ankles as though doing so would shield her from that perceptive gaze. She always felt naked to Adam. Not just stripped of clothes but of those human defenses that afforded privacy of soul. He saw inside her, just as he always had. He knew what she wanted and he wasn't going to give it to her.

"What are you trying to ask me, Georgia?" he inquired coolly. "If we'd pick up where we left off? If I'd ask you to marry me again?"

She looked away, at the fire, at her fingers knotted around her ankles. Anywhere but at him as the blood thundered in her veins and her heart leapt painfully within her breast. "...Um...I just wondered if that's what you..."

"No, it isn't," he said harshly. "If you think I'm going to bail you out of the mess you've got yourself into, think again. You want out of your marriage to Steven? Fine, get yourself out of it. Because I'll be damned if I'll let you make me the scapegoat."

"Thank you for confirming what I've suspected all along," she said, aghast at the utter desolation his reply invoked in her. "You never really wanted to marry me in the first place—God knows it took you long enough to propose—and you probably welcomed being handed an excuse to wriggle out of it, just as you're now rejoicing in the fact that someone else has stepped in to fill your shoes."

The anger that never seemed far from the surface rose up in him again. Slamming the bottle of brandy down on the table, he reached down and yanked her to her feet. She tried to shrink away, burningly conscious that he wore next to nothing, but he grasped her arm and wrenched her toward him.

"Look at me, you selfish little witch!" he raged, forcing her to acknowledge his body by pointing to his left thigh which was badly scarred. "See this? And this?" He angled his left shoulder toward her, revealing another mark, less vivid but jagged, as though the skin had torn and been left to heal without proper suturing.

Again, she tried to turn away but he wouldn't let her. "And what about this, Georgia?" he said, his voice subsiding to a savage whisper as he grabbed the fingers of her free hand and slid them along the uneven ridge of his collar bone. "That's how bone feels when it's been broken and not set properly. Not quite perfect any more."

*You're perfect to me*, she thought, at once appalled and fascinated by the feel of him. Involuntarily, her trembling hand strayed over his shoulder. His flesh was firm and resilient. Strong, invincible. Like him.

And she was a coward.

He watched her from hooded eyes and relaxed his hold on her wrist. When he spoke, his voice was hoarse though not with anger. "What sort of masochist do you think I am, Georgia, that I'd go to these lengths to avoid honoring my commitment to you?"

What was there to say in reply to such a question? And even if there were an answer, how could she have formulated it when her entire being was drowning in the sensory pleasure of touching him?

Mesmerized, she splayed her fingers over the swell of muscle on his chest. She swayed toward him, slid her hand around his waist and down the lean curve of his hips.

She leaned into him, filling herself with the scent, the texture of him; smooth, strong, vibrant. She felt the tempo of his heart beat quicken, felt the hard arousal of his response and caught her breath in delicious shock.

"Yes," Adam said, capturing both her hands in his and holding her at arm's length. "You still have the same effect on me, Georgia. Satisfied?"

"No," she whispered, dissolving into a pool of desire. "I want more."

"Well, you won't get it from me," he said. "That's Steven's ring on your finger, not mine."

Eyes glazed with hunger, she begged him. "Adam . . . please . . ."

"No," he said implacably. "I'm not going to abet you in this. You can't have it both ways, Georgia. Either you want to marry Steven, or you don't, but it's a choice you're going to make on your own. I won't let you use me as the excuse for calling things off."

She stared at him numbly. "You want me to end my engagement, but you're not willing to be named an accessory after the fact?"

"This isn't about me, it's about *you* having enough faith and trust to go after what you really want, whether or not there's any guarantee that you'll end up getting it."

Well, he could hardly have sent a plainer message! *Don't count on me to be there if you end things with Steven.*

Why was she suprised? He'd never been there for her, not really. Oh, they'd known passion and desire, but once the physical hungers had been satisfied, he'd jumped at the chance to go back to his world and left her to bury herself in hers. There'd been no real sharing of lives, none of the give-and-take she knew with Steven. And there never would be.

So why did she feel devastated all over again, when she ought to be feeling grateful that he'd at least been honest enough to tell her before she made a fool of herself a second time? Why was she allowing him to tear apart the fabric of that safe woolly cocoon that protected her so well from all the jarring, unpleasant things of life?

"Here's the brandy," she said, thrusting it into his hands and waving him away. "Take it upstairs and go back to bed. It's late, I'm tired, and I want to make an early start in the morning."

"You really intend to head back to town so soon?"

"Yes."

"You've made your choice, then?"

"Yes."

"Just like that? No giving it some more thought?"

"There's no need." She tossed her head defiantly. "You're right. I'm the only one who can decide what I want and I want to marry Steven. And I can't wait to get back to tell him that I was a fool ever to have doubted it. So I'll say goodbye now, since I'll probably be gone before you're up tomorrow."

Things didn't work out quite as neatly as she'd planned, however. For a start, Adam was awake before her the next day. Not surprising, really, considering she'd spent the night alternating between bouts of restlessness and dreams in which Adam figured so vividly that she'd half expected to find him lying beside her when she woke up.

She must have fallen at last into a sound sleep just before daybreak because she knew nothing more until the front door of the chalet opened, letting in a blast of cold air at the same time that it admitted Adam.

"No need to rush getting up," he informed her, batting snowflakes from his eyebrows. "You won't be going anywhere any time soon."

"Why not?"

"Take a look for yourself. The drifts are waist high out there and it's still coming down. We're stuck here until the weather eases off, whether or not you like."

She didn't like it. The more time she spent with him, the more he eroded her certainty that she was doing the right thing in sticking to her wedding plans. "I don't believe you," she said, draping a duvet around her, cape-fashion, and trudging to the door. "It can't be that bad."

But when she pushed past him and looked out, it was worse than bad, it was disastrous. Last night's lane had disappeared under a sloping blanket of snow that had completely buried the steps to the veranda and spread even to the firewood stacked against the wall of the building. Both cars were buried almost to the roof, with nothing but two slightly rounded humps to indicate where they were parked.

She swung back to face him, panic simmering close to the surface. "You've got to do something!"

He stood there, that damnably sexy grin on his face, lifted his broad, beautiful shoulders in a shrug. "Like what? Order the sun to shine?"

"Steven will be worried."

"Steven's already worried, and has been since you decided to cut and run up here."

"All the more reason to let him know there's no need," she said. "My mind's made up, Adam. I'm going to marry him in two weeks' time, exactly as planned."

Not a flicker of expression crossed his face. "Congratulations—but that doesn't alter the fact that we're stranded here today."

Her composure, so hard won to begin with, threatened to crack in the face of his calm acceptance of a situation that struck her as nothing short of calamitous. "I don't want to be here with you," she wailed.

"I'm not particularly enjoying the experience, either, Georgia, but howling about it isn't going to help. One thing I learned, during my enforced stay in the wilderness, is to bear with fortitude what can't be changed, and I suggest you try to do the same thing now. The snowplows will get up here in a day or two and it's not as if we don't have a roof over our heads."

"*Accept being housebound with you for a day or two?*" There was no mistaking the edge of hysteria in her voice.

"What's the matter?" he asked slyly. "Afraid you won't be able to abide by your plans?"

"No," she replied heatedly. "I'm afraid of how it will look to everyone else."

"Oh, Georgia!" He shook his head dolefully. "When did you become so conventionally hidebound that what other people might think is more important than what you know in your heart to be true?"

"Since I became the object of everyone's gossip, that's when! No one really believed I'd been the one to end our engagement." How could they have been expected to when she'd shown all the symptoms of a woman abandoned and bereft? "I remember what it was like to have people smile pityingly at me and change the subject as soon as I came within earshot of what they were saying. And I wouldn't put Steven through that for the world."

"Care for a little free advice from the man's point of view?" Adam strolled back to the fireplace and lifting down the poker hanging on the wall, stirred the embers. "He doesn't give a good goddamn what other people say. It's what his woman says, and how she looks at him when she says it, that counts. You and I could be holed up here for a month, together night and day with no one to witness anything that took place between us, but none of it would matter to Steven if he knew he could trust in your love and loyalty.''

He picked up a log and booted it with unnecessary force into place among the embers before continuing, "If, on the other hand, he had reason to suspect you were lying to him—or worse yet, lying to yourself—he wouldn't rest easy knowing you'd spent the night in a nunnery.''

"I have always been completely honest with him.''

Adam brushed one palm against the other and tugged his sweater down around his hips before turning to look at her in that direct and penetrating way of his. "Until now," he said. "Or are you going to confess that you practically begged me to make love to you last night? Or that you'd consider breaking off your engagement to him if you thought I'd be there to pick up the pieces for you?''

What disturbed her was not that he had, with his usual implacable bent for accuracy, stated the unadorned truth, but that, imprisoned here with him for another two days, she might fall prey to the same weakness again. Because no matter how firmly her head told her she'd be happier with Steven, a treacherous part of her heart yearned for Adam.

"What Steven and I might have to say to each other is none of your business," she said, scooping up her clothes and heading for the bathroom. "I'm going to get dressed so please don't come barging in until I'm finished.''

She went to brush past him but at the last minute his hand shot out. Catching her by the elbow, he dragged her close. "Do you really think you can hide your lies under a layer of clothing?" he whispered, his eyes shooting blue sparks. "Don't you know that infidelity starts in the heart, not in the flesh?"

The scent of him filled her senses, drowning her in the barely perceptible drift of after-shave mingled with snow-kissed pines. She stared at him, helpless to refute his words.

"You've already betrayed Steven, and you're going to do it again and again. And he's going to know, because every time he tries to get close to you—" He jerked his wrist and sent her off balance so that she stumbled against him, her legs meshing with his, her breasts crushed against his chest. "—like this, Georgia, he's going to know you're going through the motions only. That when he tries to kiss you, like this...."

He held her chin between thumb and forefinger, refusing to let her twist away from him. "Yes," he sneered, "that's it exactly. You'll squirm and clamp your lips together and suffer his attentions, because what if word got out that you're not honoring your conjugal obligations? Think what people would say!"

"Let go of me," she panted. "You have no right—"

He bent his head and covered her mouth with his, cutting off her breathless objection. His lips were warm and demanding and completely irresistible. Awash with desire, she sank into his embrace, every pore in her body opening to him, welcoming him.

Nothing could smother the moan of pleasure that rose in her throat; nothing could hide the hunger with which she submitted to him. And nothing, not pride or shame or outrage, could induce her to forgo the brief ecstasy he chose to bestow.

It was a kiss to remember lost ecstasy by, a kiss to start the river of regret flowing all over again. But all that mattered to her was draining every last perfect particle of pleasure from it, to hoard against a future she feared was going to be a lot less than perfect.

He took as he pleased, at his leisure. He tasted her lips, nudged them apart, slid his tongue inside her mouth, teasing and tempting her unbearably. He tasted of mountain air and freedom and passion, the sort she'd never know with any man other than him.

And then, when he had subjugated her completely, he let her go. She raised eyes glazed with desire and found herself impaled in twin fires of icy blue contempt. "And you will never ever give him what you just offered me. You will lie and pretend and offer him duty and affection. And when he takes you..."

His hand snaked from her waist to settle possessively at her breast. His knee found entry between her legs. And she cringed inside her nightshirt, knowing there was no hiding the swift rush of her response. Her nipple throbbed against his palm, the flesh of her thighs quivered and closed around his knee imploringly.

"...When he takes you," Adam ground out, "you will either close your eyes and tolerate his attentions like the dutiful wife you're determined to be, or you'll close your eyes, pretend you're with me, and let him think he's the one who brought you to orgasm."

Shock blended with desire, racing over her skin in a series of invisible jolts. "Adam... please...!"

"Either way," he said flatly, "you'll be lying to him. And sooner or later, he's going to know it." Grimacing, he let go of her and wiped his mouth with the back of his hand as if he'd tasted poison. "Go and get dressed, Georgia. The sight of you is beginning to turn my stomach."

She rushed to escape his scorching disdain. Bundling all her clothes to her breast, she ran into the bathroom.

*I cannot face him again*, she thought, pulling on her slacks and sweater with trembling, frantic hands and thrusting her feet into her high-heeled boots.

The bathroom was located down a narrow corridor that led off the main living area. Next to it was a sauna which could be accessed either from inside the cabin or by way of a door that led directly to the outside.

Under cover of the noise Adam made rattling pots and pans in the kitchen, Georgia let herself into the sauna and slid open the outside door. Bracing herself against the biting cold, she plunged into the deep snow and began to fight her way down the lane in the direction of Arne Jensen's cabin.

Almost from the start, she knew she'd set herself an impossible task. The snow ambushed her every step of the way, filling her high-heeled boots and fooling her into thinking she was on the firm surface of the lane when, in fact, she was veering into the broad ditch that ran beside it.

Once when she fell, she was barely able to struggle to her feet again. The drift was deep, insubstantial as a cloud, and climbing free taxed her strength alarmingly. But she floundered on because she had no other option. She would rather freeze to death than face Adam's unbridled scorn again.

She had covered perhaps thirty yards when he caught up with her, snowshoes strapped to his feet. "Georgia," he said, yanking her upright with ungentle hands and brushing the snow from her sweater, "I already know you're a fool. You didn't have to prove it by pulling a stunt like this."

"Leave me alone," she wept, the tears slushing unashamedly down her face and mingling with the snow. "I don't need you or your nasty remarks."

"You need me, sweet pea," he said. "You just haven't got around to admitting it yet. Where do you think you're going?"

"To Arne's," she wailed, trying unsuccessfully to shove him out of her way. "I'm going to phone Steven and he'll come and rescue me and until he gets here I'll stay with Arne who won't *molest* me all the time, the way you do."

"That's a very good idea. I should have thought of it myself. We'll go together."

"I don't want your company."

"Tough," he said. "You're stuck with it. Now quit flailing around like that before you disappear in another drift, and come back to the cabin with me. You're hardly dressed properly and even if you were, you're not going to make any headway without snowshoes."

"Quit bossing me around. You're not in the Air Force now," she snapped.

He grinned cheerfully. "We'll get some breakfast, too, while we're at it. Eggs and toast with plenty of honey to sweeten your mood."

It galled her to admit it, but he was right. She'd eaten nothing since her spinach salad the day before, and the scrambled eggs Adam whipped up with such efficiency while she changed her clothes smelled wonderful.

Fortunately, there were spare sets of just about everything in the cabin that a person might need to ward off winter: sweaters and ski pants, warm boots and jackets, socks and mittens. "Show me how to use these snowshoes," she urged Adam, the minute they'd finished eating, "and let's get going."

"In a hurry?" he inquired, lacing up his boots at irritating leisure.

"Naturally. I'm anxious to speak to Steven."

"Well, try to contain your impatience. Learning to use snowshoes isn't easy."

What an understatement! The wide-spaced, shuffling trot, that Adam managed as effortlessly as if he'd been born with the damned things attached to his feet, she managed to reproduce only as an awkward, trudging motion that set her abused muscles to screaming for deliverance. It took all her concentration and every ounce of determination for her not to collapse in a heap after the first ten minutes. And at the end of it all, Arne wasn't to be found, a fact which Georgia was slow to absorb.

"No point in battering the door down," Adam remarked, as she banged and called out to no avail. "He's not home."

"Of course he is," Georgia replied, thumping with feeble vigor. "Where else would he be in this weather?"

"Out," Adam said smugly, "which is why his cross-country skis are missing."

He pushed open the cabin door and went inside. Georgia trailed after him, dismayed. "But he's got to be here!" she wailed.

"Sorry," Adam said, sounding anything but. "I'm not a magician. I can't make him appear on command."

Georgia collapsed into the nearest chair, a straight-backed wooden rocker. "He's probably out back, bringing in more wood or something."

Adam, who'd been going over the place like some TV detective looking for murder clues, didn't so much as spare her a sympathetic glance. Instead, he placed his bare hand on the top of the cast-iron wood stove which heated the place. "Wrong again," he said. "Although the fire in this stove's ready to be replenished, there's a box of wood right here."

The way he refuted her every word had her fighting an overwhelming urge to scream with frustration. Was he ever wrong about anything? "Fine. I'll simply use the phone and leave a note explaining that I had to make an emergency call."

Adam picked up the phone receiver, listened for a moment, then dropped it back in its cradle. "You won't be doing that, either," he said, unmoved by her growing dismay. "The line's dead—probably brought down in last night's blizzard."

"You mean I'm cut off from the civilized world? Stranded here, with you?"

"Yes," he said grimly. "And if you'd stop worrying about your own problems for just a minute, you'd be bloody glad you're not stuck here by yourself. You might even find it in your selfish little heart to show a little concern for what's happened to Arne."

"He's a very capable man," she retorted sharply, refusing to acknowledge the stab of fear his comment roused in her. "He has to be, living in such isolation. And he's used to the winters up here."

"Exactly. He knows better than to leave his wood stove low on fuel. Which, as far as I'm concerned, means only one thing: wherever he is, he's been gone too long."

Despite her best efforts, Adam's concern was contagious, forcing Georgia to confront what she'd been trying to avoid. "You think something's happened to him, don't you?"

"I'd lay money on it." He drummed his fingertips on the windowsill. "Look, see if you can round up a couple of blankets, will you?"

"Go snooping through his closets, you mean? I wouldn't dream of it. It's not that cold in here."

Halfway to the back porch, Adam stopped and flung her a contemptuous glare. "Do me a favor, Georgia, and try to put aside your painfully proper upbringing long enough to help me get some sort of rescue kit ready, unless you want yet another man's future well-being on your conscience. Collect blankets, a first-aid kit, and anything else you think might be useful, and have it ready and waiting by the time I get back."

She shot out of the chair, leaving it rocking wildly. "Where are you going?" she whimpered, the prospect of being completely alone in such a hostile world infinitely worse than being stuck with Adam for company.

"To locate the sled and other emergency equipment that I'm certain a man of Arne's experience will keep on hand," he said.

The shame he aroused in her competed with what she told herself was the pure dislike he also inspired. Hatred, even, for peeling away the soft, comforting layers of her cocoon and exposing her again to all those harsh emotions she'd learned to suppress. Within twenty-four hours of Adam's return, she'd experienced rage, vulnerability, desire, fear. Dear Lord, next it would be love!

"Do you really think something serious has happened to him?" she asked, in a small voice.

"Yes," Adam said. "Better strap on those snowshoes once you find the blankets and stuff, sweet pea. If my hunch is right, we have no time to lose. Arne might be badly hurt—or dead."

# CHAPTER FIVE

IT TOOK nearly half an hour before they found any sign of the missing Arne. Half an hour of punishing effort that had Georgia drawing in great gasps of icy air that seared her lungs until she thought they'd surely collapse. But Adam plowed forward with dogged, tireless determination, towing the sled and sparing her neither a glance nor a word of sympathy or encouragement.

She was ready to drop in her tracks when suddenly, several yards ahead of her, he stopped and she knew, from the utter stillness that seemed to flow over him like a mantle, that he'd found something.

"What?" she whispered, drawing abreast of where he stood at the edge of a frighteningly precipitous gorge.

He lifted a gloved hand, pointed to a spot on the other side of the chasm, to a clump of dark evergreens. "Look over there and tell me what you see."

His tone was neutral, chillingly calm, giving away nothing of what he might be feeling. She squinted across the distance, dazzled by a fine veil of snow blowing horizontally over the lip of the hill on the far side. And then she saw them, the narrow strips of wood propped upright in the snow, their curved tips pointing skyward. "Skis," she said, turning to face him. "That's good, isn't it? It means Arne isn't far away."

But Adam had edged close to the rim of the gorge; much too close for her peace of mind. "And there's where the telephone line came down," he said, crouching to tug on a strand of ice-caked wire looping across the space to some point lower down on the opposite cliff, beyond their field of vision.

"Adam," she begged, a thread of panic cracking her voice, "please come away from the edge before you end up at the bottom."

"You're right. That wouldn't help much, would it?" He straightened, backed up a couple of feet. "How familiar are you with this area?"

"I'm not," she said. "Why do you ask?"

"Because there has to be a way across the gorge—some sort of bridge. I thought you might know where it is."

She shook her head. "No."

He shrugged, his calm unruffled. "Then we'll just have to search out Arne's tracks and follow them. You check over to the right, I'll go this way. Yell if you find something."

That he should have spotted the skis and the downed telephone line didn't surprise her. Keen observation was all part of his pilot's training. But this other side of him, this stoic refusal to bow to the elements, she'd never seen before.

"You're crazy!" she cried into the wind. "At this rate, our own tracks will soon be obliterated. We'll never find him."

"What do you suggest we do then? Abandon him to the mountain?"

"No," she said, trying to stall him because she was afraid of how much danger he was prepared to expose himself to in order to save Arne. "I just don't see the point of us risking our necks looking for someone who might not even need our help. By now, Steven will have heard the weather reports and with my not having phoned or anything, he'll realize something's wrong. He'll alert the mountain rescue unit and they'll send out a search party. How will they know where to start looking for us? We didn't leave a note or anything to indicate where we might be. I think it makes a lot more sense for us to go back to the chalet where it's safe and warm, and wait for professional help to get here.''

His gaze swept over her, colder than the wind. ''If everyone thought like you, Georgia, I'd have stayed conveniently and permanently dead, and you'd be up to your elegant eyebrows in truly critical issues—like whether people should throw rice or confetti at your wedding. Life's a real bitch, sometimes, isn't it?''

''When you're around, yes, it is,'' she retorted, hating that, with a few well-chosen words, he could uncover her weaknesses in all their stark, pathetic glory. ''But if you're determined to track down Arne, I suppose I have no choice but to go along with the idea.''

''Damned right you haven't,'' he snapped. ''Now quit wasting time and start searching. Ski tracks aren't going to show in exposed areas like this but we should find something under the shelter of the trees.''

He was right. She found them almost at once, twin grooves sliding along a narrow track that curved snakelike between the trunks and came out eventually on a small, exposed plateau about half a mile further down from the place they'd seen Arne's skis.

The gorge was narrower here, its banks jutting in toward each other to form a neck spanned by a fallen pine stripped of its branches.

''Ah!'' Nodding with satisfaction, Adam bent down and started unstrapping his snowshoes. ''Take yours off, too, Georgia,'' he ordered. ''Here's our bridge but we can't cross it wearing these. We'll have to carry them over to the other side.''

Georgia's heart almost stopped with fright. ''Adam!'' She caught at his sleeve. ''Surely you're not thinking of trusting that narrow old tree trunk to support your weight?''

''Of course. What's more, I expect you to do the same and follow right behind.''

''I can't.'' Her reply emerged on a terrified whimper. ''I'm afraid of heights, you know that.''

He spared her a brief, scornful glance before flicking her off with a jerk of his elbow. ''Then don't look down.''

How hard he'd become, how uncaring! Not that he'd even been disposed to pamper her. ''Don't make me do this, Adam, please!''

He sighed, disenchantment written all over his face. ''For crying out loud, will you put your own fears and concerns on the back burner, just this once? A man has disappeared in a blizzard. We've found his skis propped up on the far side of a canyon beyond which there's nothing but terrain that's barely passable in summer, let alone at this time of year. And whether or not you like it, I'm not about to place any faith on the ludicrous hope that a rescue helicopter will miraculously descend out of the sky in time to save him. It isn't going to happen, Georgia. Whatever sort of mess Arne's got himself into, you and I are his only way out of it. So quit whining, get those snowshoes off and sling them on your back.''

He paused just long enough to sear her with another blast of contempt from those unflinching blue eyes. ''Or else be prepared to have another man's death on your conscience—one that won't pull a resurrecting act at the eleventh hour.''

He shamed her into obeying. While she fumbled with the straps, he unloaded two ropes from the sled and looped them over his shoulder, then, when she was ready, held out his hand to her. ''Okay, grab a hold.''

The blood roared behind her eyes, a blinding red haze. "I'm scared, Adam!"

"I know." His voice softened. "I know, sweet pea. But we'll take it slow and easy. Angle your feet, like this...that's right...then just slide them forward...and look at me."

She tried. She clung to his hand, pushed one foot in front of the other. Beneath her, the tree trunk bounced gently, sending clumps of snow spiraling into the depths of the gorge.

Her gaze followed, saw nothing below but swirling space rushing up to meet her. Her heart leapt, battering fearfully at her ribs. The breath stampeded out of her, eager to escape before she plunged to her death. "...Ah...!"

*"Look at me!"*

Out of desperation, she did. In the speckled, snow-filled light, his eyes blazed, twin beacons flaring brilliant blue.

"Good woman." He nodded, gripped her hand more firmly, then swung his glance ahead again. "Now, one step at a time...."

Warmed by his encouragement, she followed him as, inch by terrifying inch, he talked her across, his words floating back and chaining her to him with hypnotic tenderness. "Easy, darling...easy...a little bit this way...just another couple of yards...there, you see...? We made it."

The deep, soft snow billowed around her ankles, welcoming her back to earth. Everything inside her trembled, her knees sagged, and she wanted nothing so much as to sink down and weep from sheer relief.

But Adam hauled her roughly upright. "Oh, no, you don't," he muttered, his warm, sweet breath fanning her face for a brief exquisite moment. "We keep right on moving. Strap the shoes on again, Georgia, and let's hit the trail."

They retraced their path, but from the opposite side of the cliff this time, and came out at the place where Arne's skis posted evidence of his having passed that way.

The snowshoes came off again. Adam edged to the lip of the gorge, leaned over with what struck Georgia as brazen defiance of the laws of gravity, and swung his head this way and that, searching. At length, he breathed, "Oh, Jesus!" and backed up to where she waited.

"He's down there," he said, forestalling her question. "Slipped, from the look of it, and landed on a ledge."

She swallowed, a great gulp of icy air. "Is he...?"

"He's not moving and from the way one leg's doubled under him, I think it's probably broken. Pity we couldn't have brought the sled across the bridge. It would have made shipping him back a whole lot easier."

All the time he talked, Adam's hands were busy uncoiling the ropes, looping one end of each around the nearest tree and securing them. That done, he attached the other end of one around his waist, coiled the spare and clipped it to his belt.

Georgia watched the whole performance in frozen disbelief, refusing to acknowledge what she knew was coming next.

"I'm going down there to tie a bowline around Arne's chest," Adam declared matter-of-factly, "then I'm coming back up and together you and I are going to haul him to the surface, because there's no way on earth I can carry him."

"Going down there?" Her question fumbled past a tongue turned suddenly thick with fear and emerged in a muffled shriek. "What do you mean, *going down there*? You can't go down there after him, Adam. You'll get yourself killed.''

His eyes glimmered with ironic laughter. "Well, that'd certainly solve a few problems for you, wouldn't it?''

"Don't joke about this!''

"Who's joking? Wish me luck, sweet pea. This isn't exactly my area of expertise.''

"...Adam...!'' Dread choked her. *Don't go*, she wanted to beg. *I can't bear to lose you again.* But to admit that would strip away the last remaining layer of self-preservation and leave her vulnerable to another onslaught of the terrible hurt she'd barely survived before.

He stood on the rim of the gorge, his broad, strong figure dark against the muted white of the snow still falling. Rooted to the spot, Georgia watched, her heart slowing to a labored, erratic thud. Her teeth sank into her lower lip deeply enough to draw pinpricks of blood, yet unable to inflict a pain sharp enough to numb the terror.

Part of her wanted to go to him, to touch him. To know one more time the feel of his body close to hers. Another part screamed, *Don't torment yourself with what you can't have. He was never right for you; he never will be. This is how things will always be with him—one high-level risk after another. It's how he gets his kicks.*

Adam turned and gave her the thumbs-up sign, something he always did in the old days before he left her for his other love, flying. And then, as suddenly as if he'd fallen off the edge of the world itself, he stepped out into space and disappeared. His lifeline vibrated against the tree trunk, twanging like a guitar string, then subsided into a series of quivering jolts.

With a cry, Georgia sprang forward, her mind empty of everything but the need to know where he was—how he was. Flinging herself down, she crawled to the very edge of the cliff, wedging herself between up-thrusting chunks of rock to preserve an illusion of safety. Slithered another few inches, opened eyes she didn't remember closing, and found herself looking down into a fallen moonscape.

Nausea rose in her throat. Boulders, pillowed in snow to disguise their bone-crushing ferocity, cradled tusks of naked rock as sharply evil as spears. And far below, the muted rush of water. Too far. The unwary body falling to those depths would travel miles before it was recovered.

Then she saw Adam, midway between heaven and hell, inert and spinning helplessly yards away from the concave wall of the canyon; a marionette with no one to pull his strings and haul him back to safety. The absolute, utter devastation to her spirit shattered her.

Only then, with everything to lose once more, did she admit to herself what she'd secretly known ever since he'd walked back into her life: there were no barriers high enough, no defences strong enough, to protect her from Adam Cabot. As easily as other men crossed from one side of the road to the other, he'd marched in and turned her life upside-down again.

Like a flower deceived by January sun into believing in false spring, her heart had begun to stir from its safe hibernation only to find winter returned with vengeful, killing cold. She wanted to die. Quietly, without fuss.

"Adam..." she mourned, pressing her face into the snow and closing her mind.

How long before sound penetrated again? One century? Two? Or when she heard the string of obscenities uttered with the fluent, violent sincerity that only an alive and very irate Adam could produce?

Trembling, she raised her head, brushed the snow from her face, and dared to look over the edge again. He was lunging at the canyon wall, propeling himself toward it with his legs, much, she supposed, as he might try to control a parachute descent. The momentum took him and slammed him against the unforgiving rock face. She heard a scream tossed away by the wind and only after realized that it had come from her lips, because his energy was directed elsewhere.

Again and again, he lunged, letting out more rope as he went, and bounced with feet extended until he'd swung clear of the bowl-shaped cavity in the canyon wall to a spot where a vein of rock projected. Arms and legs spread, he clung like a butterfly trying to anchor itself to a ledge too narrow and ice-glazed to provide footing for a flea.

To his right and perhaps six feet lower, the wider ledge where Arne lay jutted into space. From Georgia's perspective, the odds of Adam succeeding in the task he'd set himself were negligible. Neither man had a ghost of a chance of making it back up alive.

But Adam didn't know that. With the tenacity of someone prepared to defy God if he had to, he scrabbled for hold after hold, clawing with his hands, digging with his toes. And by some miracle he traversed the distance, cursing richly every slow inch of the way until he'd maneuvered himself to a point roughly eighteen inches above Arne.

Unlooping the last of his lifeline as he went, he swung down next to the injured man and landed with a crunch that echoed to the depths of the gorge. He unhitched the spare coil of rope and stooped beside the motionless body.

Heart and breath suspended, Georgia watched. And prayed he hadn't risked life and limb for nothing.

Suddenly, the line beside her hummed with tension. The scrabble of boots against rock began once more, coming closer this time as he hauled himself back to her, hand over hand, until she could almost touch him.

Concern for him outweighing fear for herself, she reached down to him. "Here, let me help you."

"Get the hell back," he rasped, his chest heaving. "You damn fool, get away from the edge before you send us both to our deaths! Take up the slack on the rope—run it around a stump or something."

She practically fell over herself rushing to comply, so busy trying to ensure his safety that she didn't notice he'd reached the surface until, suddenly, he was there beside her, swatting ice crystals from his jacket with bare, impatient hands. She opened her mouth, intending to tell him how glad she was that he'd made it back in one piece; how relieved. To her astonishment, the words drowned on a flood of tears, harsh, hopeless sobs that tore at her chest and left her throat raw.

"Hey," he said, reaching for her. "Sweet pea, it's almost over."

She grabbed blindly for his fingers and crushed them to her lips. Tasted blood and realized it was his. "Your hands," she wept, staring horrified through the endless rush of tears at his knuckles scraped raw.

"It's nothing, Georgia, just a few scratches. Stop crying."

"I can't," she sobbed, adding pitifully, "and I look so ugly when I cry!"

"You little twerp!" There was laughter in his voice. "You couldn't look ugly if your life depended on it."

"It's your life I'm concerned about," she blubbered, daubing at her tears and smearing more than she wiped. "What happened to your gloves?"

"I took them off to get poor old Arne properly trussed, then forgot to put them on again. They're down there with him, for all the good they'll do him."

A ripple of fresh dismay chased over her. "You mean, he's...?"

"Not dead, no, but I was right about his leg. It is broken, though how badly we won't know until we get him back to the cabin. He's also suffering from exposure but not as severely as he would have been if he hadn't dressed for the weather." Untying his own lifeline, he gestured to her. "Lift your arms, Georgia, so that I can tie this around you."

"What for?" she quavered, eyeing the rope with all the apprehension of a woman confronted by a boa constrictor.

"Because I'm not about to take any chances on your losing your balance and diving face-first off the cliff when you hang over the edge."

Her eyes flew wide. "You want me to hang over the edge?" she echoed in a thin voice.

"More or less. I'd do it myself but I can't be in two places at once. Someone's got to haul Arne back up and since I'm the one with all the muscle, that leaves you to take care of the easy part." He tied the last knot in the rope and gave it a tug to make sure it was secure. "Okay, you're in business."

"Isn't there another way?" she asked without hope.

"No," he said flatly, grasping Arne's lifeline in both hands, tug-of-war fashion, and digging his heels into the snow to brace himself. "All you have to do is make sure he doesn't crack his head open on those chunks of rock when I bring him up over the edge."

"Adam...!"

"I know. I'm asking a lot." He let go the rope and grazed his palm down her cheek. "But we haven't come this far to lose him now. And trust me, sweet pea, I won't let anything happen to you."

He'd always asked for more than she felt able to give. And always in that cajoling way that had her acquiescing to his demands, even when she knew doing so was nothing short of foolhardy.

But after all, it wasn't so bad, though where Adam found the strength for what he had to do, after the energy he'd already expended, was beyond her. But find it he did and brought Arne up the cliff face in half the time he'd made his own ascent. And then she forgot her own fear, too caught up in cradling the injured man's vulnerable skull and cushioning it from the slabs of granite impeding its safe passage.

"We've done it!" she cried jubilantly, as Adam gave a last heave and hauled the inert body well clear of the edge.

"Not quite." He knelt beside Arne, his expression grave, and searched for the man's pulse. "We still have to get him across that bridge." He looked up, impaling her in that irresistible blue gaze. "Are you up to it, Georgia? Can I count on you?"

"You could always count on me," she whispered, a wave of regret washing over her. "It was I who couldn't count on you."

"Yes, you could," he said softly. "You just gave up on me too soon, that's all."

"Better not waste time taking him to his place," Adam decided, after they'd navigated the bridge and had Arne loaded on the sled. "His stove was nearly out this morning and it must be cold as a witch's thorax in there by now."

But the Drake chalet was warm and snug, even though the fire had died to little more than a handful of glowing ashes. While Adam coaxed it to new life with fresh kindling and logs, Georgia searched out extra quilts and two hot water bottles she found under the sink in the bathroom.

"Good." Adam nodded approval when he saw. "Fill them, will you, while I strip off his outdoor clothing and take a look at his leg?" And to Arne, who'd regained befuddled consciousness, "You're going to have to bite the bullet on this, pal. It's frontier surgery at its most primitive, and it's going to hurt like hell."

Adam had not exaggerated. Hearing the injured man's moans, Georgia cringed. "Here, Arne," she murmured, tipping an inch of brandy into a cup and holding it to his lips, "maybe this will help."

"You missed your calling," Adam told her. "You make a great nurse."

*As you*, she could have said, observing the gentle sureness of his touch as he straightened the limb and bound it to a makeshift splint, *would have made a wonderful doctor—and how much different things might have turned out between us, then*.

With uncanny telepathy, they worked as a team to stabilize the patient, anticipating each other's need for assistance. After they each showered and changed into dry clothes, it was past five and already dark. And suddenly, there was nothing to keep them busy anymore; nothing to cushion the awareness vibrating between them.

"Just as well we didn't wait for that rescue unit," Adam remarked, staring out of the window at the blowing snow. "They aren't going to make it up here today—or tomorrow, either, at this rate. Another eight inches must have fallen since this morning."

Trapped in the same tension that drove him to rap out a restless tattoo against the frost-etched glass, Georgia didn't reply. Morning was a distant memory in a day that seemed to have lasted hours beyond its normal time span. She had done things—dangerous, life-and-limb-threatening things that she'd have thought no one could persuade her to do.

She had seen Adam save a man's life, had put her own in jeopardy to help him do so. He had asked her to trust him and, because there'd been no other choice, she had. And he had not let her down. Why, after all that, was it so difficult to talk to him now?

"Lucky it's just a simple fracture." Unlike her, Adam seemed driven to break the silence between them. "The leg should heal well enough, once the bone's been properly set."

She nodded mutely, but of course he didn't know that because he was making a determined point of not looking at her. Even though night had obliterated the world outside, he continued to gaze through the window as though mesmerized by the view.

Unhindered, she feasted her eyes on his tall, spare elegance, his narrow hips, the black hair that dared to curl at the nape of his neck, and wondered how she could possibly have thought she could ignore how sexy he was.

The admission opened the door to a flood of memories that had been shut away for a very long time. So many things she'd missed, private things that only a lover could have known. The texture of his skin, velvet stretched taut over steel. The way his lashes drooped to hide the fire in his blue eyes just before he lost the battle with desire. His voice in her ear, whispering outrageous, intimate words of love and encouragement as he taught her what passion was all about. The scent of him, quintessentially male, erotic, tantalizing.

"Got any more of that soup you made for Arne?" Abruptly, he swung around and caught her in the act of staring. "I don't know about you, but I'm starving."

*So am I, Adam!* she thought wildly. Dampening her lips with the tip of her tongue, she said, "It was just consommé out of a can—nothing very filling, I'm afraid—but I could broil a couple of steaks and make a salad."

"Better yet. Need any help?"

"No." She shied away, terribly afraid of where her errant thoughts might lead her if he came any closer. "No, thanks, I can manage."

He shrugged. "Then I'll raid the wine cupboard. Steven's not the kind of guy to leave it unstocked."

*Steven.* It had been hours since she'd spared him a thought. Worse, straining to picture him in her mind's eye now, she found his features blurred and unfocused, usurped by the sharper image of the man she'd spent fifteen months trying to forget.

"This ought to do." Apparently not nearly as discombobulated by her presence as she was by his, Adam set a bottle of Bordeaux on the counter and searched out wineglasses and corkscrew. "Care for a snort while you cook?"

"I'll wait," she said. She had eaten nothing since breakfast and wine on an empty stomach could quickly lead to the disastrous impairment of good judgment. Any number of unwise declarations were liable to fall from lips loosened by alcohol.

"Suit yourself." He poured a glass and wandered over to the fireplace with it. "How about some music?"

"If it won't disturb Arne."

"Not likely. With all the brandy you poured into him, he'll sleep the clock around. What would you like to hear?"

*Anything but that sexy drawl of yours*, she almost screamed. Good God, couldn't he *feel* the tension that sent goose bumps prickling over her scalp? "Anything—I don't care—Louis Armstrong."

"Good choice. There's a whole slew of his stuff to choose from." He whistled softly, tunelessly, and selected CDs. Armstrong's singular, unmistakable voice, half gravel, half honey, flowed through the room in a string of timeless favourites; *Stormy Weather*, *Kiss of Fire*, *Dream A Little Dream Of Me*.

*Bad choice*, Georgia decided, axing a tomato in half with a chef's knife as the lyrics wove spells around her and planted all manner of cockeyed ideas in her head. "How do you like your steak, Adam?"

He slouched in the armchair, legs stretched out in front of him, eyes closed, glass of wine dangling negligently from one hand except for the times he raised it to his lips. Supremely comfortable, supremely relaxed. She hated him.

Satchmo understood. *I'll Be Glad When You're Dead, You Rascal You*, he crooned.

"I said, how do you like your steak, Adam?"

He turned his head and pinned her in a lazy gaze. "You know how I like my steak, Georgia. Don't pretend you've forgotten."

"Rare," she fumed.

He smiled. "Right. Just a little this side of blue."

"Then you'd better get yourself to the table. Dinner's just about ready and I'm not serving it to you on your lap."

He ambled across the room, endearingly rumpled. "Are you this crabby with Steven, too," he inquired, pouring her a glass of wine and topping up his own, "or is it the one thing you reserve especially for me?"

"Shut up," she said ungraciously. "I want to listen to the music."

Right on cue, Louis gave his best to *I Only Have Eyes For You*.

Across the table, Adam raised his glass. "What shall we toast?"

She chewed her lip and tried to dig up something bland and innocuous. "How about, to having survived the day?"

"It isn't the day I'm worried about," Adam said, capturing her in a watchful, unblinking gaze.

And she knew then what was causing the tension between them, why they couldn't talk like normal people sharing a meal. He was right. It wasn't the day. It was the endless hours of the coming night.

And the fact that a man with a broken leg occupied one of the only two beds in the place.

# CHAPTER SIX

AT FIRST, she didn't know what disturbed her. She lay in her half of the bed and let her eyelids flicker open, surprised to discover she'd slept at all. Instantly and acutely alert, she waited, listening.

Nothing. Even the wind had died, leaving the blackness of night to fold thickly around the chalet except where a sliver of moonlight pierced the little round stained-glass window, high up near the apex of the roof.

And then she heard it again, the noise that had jarred her awake: unintelligible mutterings that sank into a gentle moan. The sort of sound a man in pain might make, but much too close to be Arne's.

Suspicious, she tensed.

"We can build a barrier of pillows between us, if it'll make you feel better," Adam had offered, in response to her somewhat hysterical reaction at the idea of their sharing the bed in the loft, "and pretend we're in a remake of that old Clark Gable movie."

Feeling thoroughly silly, she'd replied stiffly, "That won't be necessary, provided we agree to respect each other's space."

Later, as he'd divested himself with unselfconscious efficiency of everything but a pair of briefs that truly merited the description, she'd found her gaze drawn again to the ragged scar running between his left knee and groin.

Misinterpreting her strangled gasp, he'd shaken his head. "Your virtue has never been safer," he said with a yawn, stretching and showing a great deal of broad muscular chest in the process. "I'm practically comatose with exhaustion." And to prove it, he'd collapsed on his half of the bed and fallen asleep almost immediately.

That, though, had been hours ago. Had she been wrong to believe he'd honor their agreement until morning?

She lay on her side, rigid as a barge pole, precariously balanced so near the edge of the mattress that a deep sigh would have been enough to topple her to the floor.

It had taken hours before she, too, had slept. Uncomfortably cold hours, enough that, had it been anyone other than Adam Cabot lying next to her, she'd have cuddled up to his sleeping body and stolen a little of its warmth. But given her predisposition to dissolve into a heap of willing flesh the instant she came within touching range of him, she resisted the urge.

Cautiously, she rolled onto her back, prepared to voice her outrage in no undertain terms if Adam attempted to ambush her under cover of night.

"...Aagh..." From the other half of the bed, the quiet moan rose again, then sank into a whisper. "...can't get back to... Firefly...no time..."

Eyes gradually adjusting to the gloom, Georgia clutched the feather duvet to her chin and raised her head. On his half of the bed, Adam lay in a tangle of covers, his breathing punctuated by sighs that seemed to tear his soul apart.

Suddenly, he hunched over, grasped his scarred leg with both hands and dragged it close. *"Don't touch me!"* The words bounced to the rafters, angry, authoritative, followed by others she didn't understand. Garbled syllables of some foreign language, brittle with consonants.

"Adam?" Georgia reached out and placed a tentative hand on his shoulder. His flesh burned to the touch.

He jerked as if she'd stabbed him, moaned again, then said urgently, "Firefly, Firefly, this is Red Dog. Do you read me, Firefly?"

At once fascinated and horrified, Georgia rose to one elbow and leaned over him. "Adam," she whispered again, "are you all right?"

"The bloody cold is enough to kill a man, you know," he informed her conversationally. "Better get a move on if I'm going to save this poor slob."

But she could feel the heat emanating from him and what he muttered made no sense. "You're dreaming," she said. "Wake up, Adam."

"...losing control, Firefly...*oh, Jesus...*" He kicked at the duvet, sending it flying in the air. Another sigh moaned through the night, and by the moon's pale glimmer she saw tears clustered along his lashes. "...Georgia..." he murmured, tormentedly. "...Georgia, please...wait...."

It was more than she could bear, to lie this close to him and not comfort him. Feeling his pain, aching for his misery, she reached out and slipped an arm around him. "Hush," she whispered, pillowing his head at her breast. "I'm here."

Why couldn't she have taken the sweetness of the moment in stride? Accepted it as the unlooked-for gift it was, a little secret treasure to hoard to herself through all the years of the rest of her life, and let that be enough? She might have, could have, if only he hadn't displayed in sleep the sort of stunning vulnerability he'd never deign to expose when he was awake. It was that which undid her.

He turned to her in the night, sighed with heart-breaking relief, and left her craving more. Hunger ravaged her, a staggering thing that melted her inner resources to a pool of liquid wanting. Wanting his kiss, his touch, his possession; the feel of his naked body pressed to hers, within hers. Wanting him so badly, she could have screamed.

The nightmare had become so familiar that it had almost lost the power to traumatize him. As long as he didn't resist, didn't try to alter its course, it always passed and eventually set him free. He'd wake up, devastated all over again perhaps, but alive. And given life, anything was possible, even the miracle of finding his way back to Georgia.

But this time was different. The gremlins were more determined, the remembered agony more acute. The sense of utter helplessness he'd known as the jet spiraled out of control grabbed hold of him and wouldn't let go. The roaring filled his ears and he felt himself spinning...nosediving through eternity.

Except this time, it was worse than usual. There was someone with him, the Norwegian who lived next door to the Drakes on the mountain, and all that stood between the old man and certain death was Adam Cabot in all his frailty.

Muscles locked, he anticipated the end, braced himself for the shattering impact of blasting through the earth's crust and into the vast jaws of hell. And instead found himself buoyed up by clouds, led by the soft, hypnotic beat of drums to a place beside which Eden paled.

There were flowers all around him, filling his senses with their perfume. Breezes riffling through his hair and caressing his cheek. "A man can take any amount of this sort of punishment," he murmured, burrowing deeper into the sweet warmth and wrapping his arms around it.

"Adam...?" The voice he'd never thought to hear again beckoned to him, drawing him closer to paradise.

Cool fingers slipped down his face and the drums he'd heard became her heartbeat. It was the dream ending he'd always hoped for and never realized.

She was all around him, warm, alive. Just him and her, traveling across time and space to find each other again. *You're still dreaming*, he told himself, denying cognizance long enough to allow the weakening of resolutions his daytime self had promised to honor.

Reaching into the night, he found her. Closed his hands around her softness, rolled to his side and drew her against him, crushing her sweet breasts against his chest, tangling her legs with his.

If he could simply hold her, touch her, kiss her, he thought hazily, it would be enough. But where previously the destructive power of the dream had sapped the life from him, this time it transmuted into a raging passion that brought him fully awake even as it engulfed him.

He ran his hands over her body, shaping her hips, her waist, her ribs. He moved back to find her breasts, cupped them in his hands and felt them bloom, full and eager, against his palms.

He wanted to savor the moment, make its small perfection suffice, and not think about tomorrow until its bleakness stared him in the face. But she rose up to meet him, her mouth hot and sweet on his. After that, small perfection wasn't enough.

No longer befuddled by dreams, he consigned finesse to the same unhappy fate as restraint. Shoving haphazardly at the folds of her nightgown until nothing separated her from him but humming anticipation and the beguiling fragrance of her skin, he pulled her on top of him.

The old Georgia, her flame restored, dropped her head, and whispered his name into his mouth. Her hands, restless, magical, told him what he wanted to know; led him to the destination he'd never thought to find again, in a silent ritual that required no words.

He held her poised above him, petitioned her with a nudging of his taut flesh, and felt her lustrous quiver of acceptance. Pulling her close once more, he held her hips and sank deep into the sleek warmth of her.

To say they fit together as comfortably as a pair of old shoes would have demeaned the splendor, but the fact was she came to him easily, with flawless grace and familiarity. Softly, deliciously, accommodating his tempered strength. Driven beyond caution or conscience, he capitulated to the primitive rhythm driving him, possessed by the stolen ecstasy of the moment.

Morning came with crystalline brilliance, exposing all their nocturnal self-deceptions for what they really were: an excuse to indulge their sexual greed for each other at the expense of someone else, namely Steven. Never in a thousand years, no matter what the provocation, would he betray Georgia as she had betrayed him.

Sunlight bounced from the snow piled up on the outside window sill to the unrelenting candor in Adam's eyes as they encountered hers across the breakfast table.

Unable to face him, Georgia threw on her jacket and went out to the veranda. Soon after, he followed and came to stand next to where she leaned against the railing. Together, they stared down the lane, as if, by doing so, they could conjure up the means of their escape from one another.

At length, he spoke. "Look, about last night, I didn't intend for us—"

"I know. Neither did I."

"I wasn't prepared." He cleared his throat. "Should we worry that you might be—?"

"No," she said, knowing what he was asking, and knowing that, once again, she couldn't tell him, even though the timing could not have been worse and it might well turn out that they had every reason to worry. Whatever else her sins, entrapment wasn't one of them.

"How can you be sure? Surely you and Steven—?"

"Of course. I saw a doctor." She drew in a sharp breath and let the lie fall with only a slight twinge of conscience. It was, after all, such a small deception in the greater scheme of things. "We decided I'd take care of...that."

With a sudden, abrupt movement, Adam got up and paced the width of the veranda. "There's something obscene about this conversation," he said harshly, staring out at the blinding morning. "We don't know how to communicate with each other any more. We talk—but we're not in touch."

It struck Georgia that, depending on one's definition of communication, they'd managed to get in touch rather well in the night just past. It did not seem a politic time to say so, however; the brilliance of the morning allowed for none of the self-delusion arrived at under cover of dark. They had made a terrible mistake. The best they could hope for now was to effect immediate damage control to make sure no one else paid for their utter lack of judgment.

"Yes," she said, hating the awkwardness that existed between them, and wishing she could blame him for it. But the truth of the matter was that, from the moment he'd rested his head at her breast and uttered her name in that heartbroken voice, she had aided and abetted his every move.

She could have stopped him. All it would have taken was a word, a sign from her. Whatever else his failings, Adam was not a man to coerce a woman against her will. But she had allowed herself to see past the dark good looks, the broad, charming, utterly seductive grin, to the private hurts he guarded so jealously, and that had been a fatal mistake.

It had stripped her of her resistance as little else could have, leaving her at the mercy of the desire that trailed through her, hot and sweet as syrup, to converge in pulsing expectation between her thighs. And now she had to live with the knowledge of what she'd done.

Adam paced back to her, his tall, loose-limbed frame crowding her into a corner of the veranda. "I've always believed guilt to be a waste of energy," he said, "but that doesn't mean I'm without regret or remorse—for things I couldn't help, and for some that I encouraged."

"I don't want your regret or your remorse," she told him. "I don't want anything from you."

"The trouble is," he went on, sweeping aside her words as if they hadn't been uttered, "that, unlike money, time is not a negotiable commodity. I can't go back, and neither can you. Our only choice lies in which direction we choose to march forward."

"And I have made that choice," she lied, because she had no other option. A sequence of events had been set in motion months ago and it was more than she could face to bring them to a halt. "I've made my bed and I'm perfectly prepared to lie on it."

Adam teetered back and forth on his heels. "An unfortunate choice of metaphor under the circumstances, Georgia," he said mockingly. "Do I take that to mean you intend to go ahead and marry Steven, with him none the wiser for your... little lapse?"

"What purpose would it serve to tell him, except to hurt him unbearably? It's not as if what..." Swallowing to relieve the sudden dryness in her throat, she tried again. "What happened between us last night—"

"When we made love?" he supplied.

"Love?" She looked at him searchingly.

His gaze flickered away. "All right. Had sexual intercourse. Does that sound better?"

"It doesn't sound real," she said. "I have difficulty believing it actually happened."

"Oh, it happened all right," he assured her, "but if you want to pretend it didn't, that's your business. In fact, I'll make it easy for you. Once we get back to town and I've tied up a few loose ends, I shall go away."

If he had ripped out her heart and ground it beneath his heel, the agony could not have been worse.

Something of the pain she endured must have shown on her face because, after a moment during which she felt his gaze return to her, he said, "I do not like to think I'm the sort of man who goes around hurting other people, Georgia, yet I seem to make a habit of hurting you. This time when I leave, it really will be for good."

She would hurt for the rest of her life, she thought numbly. The skill would lie not in surviving it, but in concealing it. "Where will you go?"

She felt rather than saw him shrug. "Why do you care?"

*Because I can't bear not knowing where you are, who you're with.* "I was thinking about your grandmother. Won't she miss you?"

"Probably not as much as I'd like to think. We're all dispensable, I've found. She compensated for my absence by turning to her friends, her charities—just as you turned to Steven." He flexed his shoulders and looked away. "She can meet me in other places. Piper Landing isn't the center of the universe."

Unbidden, another intrusive question she had no business asking popped out of Georgia's mouth. "Will you ever get married, do you think?"

His reply devasted her. "Sure," he said carelessly, scooping a handful of snow from the veranda railing into a ball and hurling it out into the brilliant sunshine. "I might also take up ballet."

His glib response more brutally exposed their shared night together for what it had really been: sexual gratification, pure and simple. Marriage, whether his or someone else's, still was not something he took seriously. As for her—her weakness was slightly less despicable than her promiscuity.

She wanted to weep for the things she'd forfeited: her first love, her innocent belief in happy endings, her lost child. Her fighting spirit.

How typical of what she'd become, to weep and wring her hands over those losses, instead of striving to repair them. And how utterly cruel to have compounded the sin of indolence with cheap, shabby self-indulgence.

Nothing less than the need to flagellate her conscience prompted her next question. "Was there ... anyone else for you ... while you were away, I mean?"

He fixed her in a cool stare. "I don't think you have any right to ask that, do you?"

She flushed. "You're right. It's none of my business."

But saying that, believing it even, didn't prevent the thoughts from swirling in her mind. *Who had nursed him back to health? Wiped away the sweat when the fever took hold, held his hand when the pain engulfed him? Bathed him, comforted him, during the long months of his recovery?*

He placed his hand flat on the door leading back inside the chalet and pushed it open. "I expect they'll clear the roads today and we'll be free to move out of here. I'll find out from Arne what I can do at his place before we leave, to make things a bit easier for him when they let him out of hospital. Even a man of his indomitable self-reliance will find a cast on his leg something of a liability, at least for a little while."

It was noon when she heard the grind of the snowplow coming up the lane, and half an hour after that before Steven arrived in the four-wheel-drive Jeep his family used to negotiate the mountain roads during the winter.

"I am so glad to see you," he said, his voice and eyes brimming with the sincerity of his love as he ran up the steps to where she waited to greet him. "I have missed you dreadfully."

She went into his open arms and hid her face against his shoulder, weighed down by the enormity of the wrong she had done him. "Steven," she choked, "there's something you should know."

He lifted her chin and looked gravely into her eyes. "You are safe and I am here to take you home if you are ready to come. I do not need to know anything else," he said with unwavering certainty.

She knew then that she could not destroy him with an admission of her infidelity unless he asked her point-blank about it, something he would never insult her by doing.

"I thought you would never get here," she said, the tears clogging her voice. "I've missed you, too."

He held her away from him and gazed at her searchingly. "Have you?"

"More than I can tell you." Oh, how convincingly her tongue shaped a truth cloaked in deceit!

"And you're ready to come home again?"

"Yes!" she cried, the desperation almost surfacing. "As soon as possible. I never should have come here to begin with."

"Your family will be glad. Your mother—"

"My mother must be a basket case!"

He laughed. "Just about. She must have phoned at least twenty times in the last two days." He lifted his eyebrows questioningly. "I told her there was nothing to worry about. Was I right?"

What sort of person would it take to crush the hopes he held out to her with the same unspoken plea that a starving child might offer an empty plate? Someone more honest, more honorable? More courageous? It didn't signify; what mattered was that she was not that sort of person. "You were right."

"Do you think," he said, touching her cheek lightly, "that you could smile when you say that? I have always found your smile so lovely."

She thought her face would shatter into a thousand pieces. "Oh, Steven," she said, turning and pressing a kiss to his palm, "you are so much more than I deserve. How would I have managed this last year without you?"

"Who cares? The situation never arose." He cleared his throat. "When do you want to start back to town?"

"As soon as we've taken care of our casualty."

"Casualty?"

"Yes. Arne broke his leg trying to find where his telephone line came down."

A change swept over Steven's face, a subtle relaxation of the little grooves of worry pinching his features. "Ah, so that's what you were going to tell me," he said, following her inside to where the old man lay with his bad leg propped on a rolled-up duvet. "I confess I was a bit concerned when I couldn't get through to you on the phone, but it never occurred to me there'd been an accident. Good thing Adam was here to lend a hand." He hesitated fractionally, casting a quick glance around the room. "Where is he, by the way?"

"At my house," Arne supplied, unwittingly adding authenticity to the overall deception being perpetuated.

"*Ja*, he knows that winter in the mountains is not a time to leave a place alone."

Was that relief that briefly rolled over Steven's face before he could mask it? Fresh shame rose up in Georgia, bitter as poison. "He needs to get to a hospital so that the bone can be set properly," she said, rushing to fill the silence before guilt had her spilling out a confession. "Can you take him?"

"Yes." With the selfless capability that was his trademark, Steven sized up the situation and took charge. "There's room for you to lie in the back of the Jeep, Arne, but it's a good thing the new hospital at Fiddler's Run is open because I'm afraid you'd find it a long, rough ride all the way back to Piper Landing. Will you come with us, Georgia?"

"No. I'll stay here, pack my stuff, and clean up the chalet so that we're able to leave as soon as you get back."

"That makes more sense, now that I think about it," Steven said. "The road's pretty clear and the sanding crews are out, but a cold front has moved in and icy conditions are expected once the sun goes down. I'd rather you weren't driving after dark, love, though we could, of course, wait until tomorrow if you'd rather."

"No," she said hastily. "Let's head home today."

*As soon as possible*!

She wanted to put the last two days behind her for ever. No reminders, no lingering at the scene of the crime. She would never come to this place again as long as she lived.

Adam heard the sound of gears shifting on the last incline to the Drake place, threw more logs in the wood stove and poured himself another snort from the contents of the stone crock he'd found in Arne's kitchen cupboard. Cold, colorless, and definitely alcoholic, it was evil stuff, strong enough to take paint off the wall and even numb the permanent ache in his thigh. But not quite potent enough to erase last night's memories.

One good thing about the land of the midnight sun was that it limited the hours in which dreams, as well as nightmares, could creep up under cover of dark and take a man by surprise. Dreams were trouble, distorting reality, impairing judgment, and raising a person's hopes to impossible heights.

The door on the cuckoo clock hanging on the wall sprang open. Twelve times the damn bird chirped, enough to drive a man to drink if his conscience hadn't chased him there first. Adam tilted the glass, squinted at the bead of liquor rolling smoothly down the side, and contemplated his next move.

Give it another hour, he figured, and they'd be gone, back to their socially correct wedding and the rest of their socially correct lives. Then he could go pick up his own stuff and drive back to civilization himself. Maybe bypass Piper Landing and head straight for Vancouver, city of bright lights and faceless, nameless, available women.

On the other hand, he could stay right where he was and get thoroughly plastered. Of the two choices, the second presented fewer risks and required a lot less effort.

Everything, it seemed, was conspiring to keep Georgia prisoner at the site of her downfall. First, Steven was taking much longer than she'd expected to deliver Arne to the hospital, then, when she had her suitcase packed and ready to load in the trunk, she realized that although the lane might be clear, her car was still buried in snow.

It would take a good half hour to dig it out, and waiting for Steven to do the job would prolong the agony of delay, not to mention increase the likelihood of Adam's showing up again before she was gone.

The snow shovel she found was one of those wide, unwieldy things designed for masculine brawn. Meant to be pushed rather than heaved, it probably worked very well on the paved residential driveways for which it was intended, but it balked at the unevenness of the terrain around the chalet. Sheer annoyance at the repeated obstacles she kept encountering was all that gave Georgia the energy to persevere with the damned thing.

"Planning to dig mine out, too, while you're at it?"

She had not heard Adam return. Startled, she swung around with the shovel at shoulder height, missing his head by a matter of inches. "When did you get back?" she demanded ungraciously.

He grinned. "About eleventy-seven seconds ago."

A faint whiff of something vaguely alcoholic drifted from him. She wrinkled her nose fastidiously. "You've been drinking! You smell like a still."

He rounded on her with startling, furious speed. "And you sound like a nagging wife," he raged in a low voice. "I am not, however, your henpecked husband—nor am I nearly as drunk as I'd like to be. Booze is not one of my weaknesses."

"Why couldn't you have stayed away another hour?"

He whistled tonelessly, banking his anger. "Gee, Georgia, you don't sound any more pleased to see me now than you did when I miraculously came back from the grave. Kind of makes me wonder why you ever bothered with me in the first place. Could it be this is the only way you can show a man you love him?"

"If what I feel for you is love," she said, her heart splintering in ruins at the deadly thrust he aimed at it, "then God help me! I never want to see your face again after today."

He shucked off his jacket. "In that case," he said, wrestling the snow shovel away from her, "allow me to speed you on your way. You'll be here until next week at your present rate of progress."

It galled her that he made the task look so easy. It disturbed her that he looked so utterly gorgeous. It appalled her that the sight of him, drunk or sober, was enough to turn her liquid with longing.

She was ready to scream with frustration. Three days ago, she had been in control of her destiny, looking forward to a nice wedding, a nice husband, a nice life. Dull, by some people's standards perhaps, but oh, so safe. How could it all have changed so dramatically in such a short time?

"Steven's here, you know," she said, as though the mention of his name would be enough to ward off the evil spell under which she'd fallen.

"I figured as much."

"He's taken Arne to the hospital."

Adam halted his efforts long enough to register his surprise. "In Piper Landing? That's a six-hour, round-trip drive."

"There's a new hospital opened at Fiddler's Run Ski Resort in the next valley. He should be back here any time now."

"I should have figured something like that." Adam resumed his attack on the snowbank. "It's not Steven's style to abandon a maiden in distress."

"Unlike you!" she said sharply.

That was her second mistake. The first was in not having believed Adam when he said he wasn't nearly as drunk as he'd like to be. Indeed, the speculative gaze he brought to bear on her told her that he was completely sober.

"Would you care to explain that remark, Georgia?" he asked softly.

"No," she mumbled, turning away to hide her confusion. "I mean, there's nothing to explain. Suffice it to say that, as I told you the other night, the alacrity with which you seized the chance to escape the marriage trap left some people unconvinced it was my decision to call off our wedding."

Another in her growing list of little white lies and blatant misrepresentations, but who was keeping score? No one but Steven knew she'd been pregnant at the time Adam had left, and he would never tell.

But Adam was even more perceptive than she'd given him credit for. He closed iron fingers around her wrist and spun her back to face him, bringing her up sharply against the unyielding strength of his chest. From a distance, they might have been lovers about to embrace.

Fragrant with mountain air and caraway-flavored liqueur, his breath winnowed over her face. "Why do I feel as if the two of us are involved in a game, Georgia," he murmured, his gaze seeming to bore into that corner of her mind where she hoarded all her secrets, "but that you're the only one who knows the rules?"

She didn't know how she'd have answered him if, at that moment, the Jeep hadn't swung around the bend in the lane. "Please let go before Steven sees you clutching me like this and wonders what's been going on behind his back," she said calmly. "I would not like him to jump to the right conclusions and question the wisdom of marrying me. As for games, I grew tired of them about the same time that I grew tired of you."

Adam dropped her as if he'd been shot. Quickly, completely. "If I thought you really were the unfeeling bitch you pretend to be, I could quickly learn to despise you—and I certainly pity Steven."

Without another word she tore herself free from the scorn in his eyes and turned to greet her fiancé. Opaquely wary, Steven's glance fickered to Adam, then back again to her. He touched her elbow. "What's going on, Georgia?" he asked.

# CHAPTER SEVEN

"NOTHING." Hearing the breathlessness in her voice, Georgia felt sure Steven must correctly ascertain it stemmed from guilt. "When can we leave?"

"As soon as you're ready." He indicated her suitcase with her car keys slung carelessly over the handle, and the box of food she'd cleared out of the refrigerator. "Is this everything?"

"Except for my jacket and purse."

"I'll get them."

"No!" She had not meant to sound so shrill but, unnerved by the raking scorn in Adam's eyes, she didn't know which was worse: leaving him alone to say God knew what to Steven, or being left alone with him herself. "What I mean," she added apologeticaly, "is that I know where I left them, so I'll do it."

"All right." Steven nodded slightly and picked up her keys. "Then I'll start your car while you're gone. It'll take a while for the engine to warm up."

She raced inside the chalet, wanting above all else to short-circuit any sort of conversation between the two men. In his present mood, Adam was dangerous and liable to say anything.

Her coat lay over the back of one of the kitchen chairs but it took precious moments for her to locate her purse which she'd left upstairs, in the loft where she had spent the night with Adam.

Without premeditation, she sank again to the bed and laid her face on the cool, smooth duvet. The night...and Adam. Would she ever separate them in her mind?

That was, of course, the real reason she and Steven had never made love. During the day, her impersonation of a woman caught up in passion would be too apparent, and the nights were not for sharing. They were the times when she took out her hoard of memories and relived them. How could she contemplate marrying one man when another invaded her nights?

Below the window, her car horn tooted a reminder that the afternoon was passing quickly toward evening. Scooping up her purse from the little pine dresser beside the bed, she hurried down to the front door again just as Adam's voice floated through the still air.

"If you wanted to prove something by sending me up here, Steven old buddy," she heard him say, "you succeeded. We're not rivals in love. The lady is all yours. Take her with my blessing."

He was loading her suitcase in the trunk of her car as he spoke, and Steven stood beside the driver's door, with his back to her. She did not catch his reply but whatever it was, it made Adam laugh. That they could attempt a joke at such a time alienated her to the point of almost hating both of them.

"That's very sporting of you, Adam, I'm sure," she snapped, marching down the steps and sweeping past him, "but I am not some inanimate trophy to be handed back and forth between friends."

"You give a pretty good imitation of one at times," he drawled.

"Georgia, love!" Steven swung around in consternation. "You've got it all wrong. Adam didn't mean that the way it sounded."

"Yes, I did," Adam said. "Every word."

Temper flaring and emotions raw, Georgia consigned to perdition what was left of her socially correct, scrupulously moral upbringing. "Drunken sot!" she spat, sweeping past him with a killing glare and climbing into the driver's seat. "Horse's ass!"

Her last impression, snatched through the rearview mirror as the car skidded down the lane, was of Steven shaking his head in bewilderment—and Adam leaning on the handle of his snow shovel, doubled up with mirth.

From the day she had moved in, her cottage had been her haven. She loved its honey-colored oak floors, the view of the river from its paned windows, its curving staircase and brass light fixtures. But most of all, she loved its absence of painful nostalgia.

There was nothing of Adam in this house. No recalling his filling the doorway with his height, or slouching with lean, economical grace to scoop up the morning newspaper. No mental image of him sitting across from her in the sunny, south-facing window of the breakfast nook. No memory of him stretching out beside her in the four-poster bed upstairs, his hand toying with her hair or his mouth igniting her passion.

Yet when she let herself in the front door on her return from the chalet, he came in with her, if not in the flesh then undeniably in spirit. He took up residence with such swift ease that she knew she'd only been fooling herself in believing she'd ever been free of him. He'd been lurking in the shadows all along.

She carried her suitcase up the stairs and while she unpacked, listened to the calls on her telephone answering machine. Predictably enough, most of them were from her mother whose distress became more pronounced with each message.

"Georgia, I just spoke to Steven. He told me where you are and I'm terribly worried. Why couldn't you have come to your family, instead of running away? Call me the minute you get back, dear, please!"

"I had hoped to hear from you before now, Georgia. Your father and I are very concerned."

"This is unforgivable, Georgia. What am I supposed to tell people when they ask where you are? The wedding's only fifteen days away."

"I spoke to Steven again this morning. He puts on a brave front, but I see Adam Cabot's fine hand in all of this. Don't you think Steven deserves better than to be put through such anxiety at this late date?"

Last, in the unlikely event that Georgia had somehow misunderstood her mother's concern, came Samantha's dire prediction. "This is your sister." As if there was any mistaking those righteous tones! "Just in case you haven't yet realized it, Adam Cabot is nothing but trouble. He's incapable of giving a woman what she needs and you're driving Mother to an early grave with all your last-minute nonsense. If you let Steven slip through your fingers, you'll regret it for the rest of your life. You'll end up a lonely old woman with no one to take care of you and it will be nothing less than you deserve. I cannot believe you're gambling with your future like this. You must be mad."

*Adam nothing but trouble?* Undoubtedly, Georgia thought, trailing discarded clothes on the floor from bedroom to bathroom. But, *unable to give a woman what she needed?*

She filled the old cast-iron, claw-footed tub, added a lavish capful of perfumed bath oil, then lowered herself into the water. Fragrant ribbons of steam wound protectively about her, attempting to block the sensory memories that sliced through her mind with unparalleled clarity, but they outmaneuvered her from the start.

She lifted one foot, absentmindedly examined its rose-tipped toes, and acutely relived the touch of Adam's hand as it swept the length of her thigh.

What he gave her covered the entire spectrum of human emotion. With him she knew grief, ecstasy, pain, joy. He brought her fully alive again, tempering regret with hope.

*Gambling with her future*? She soaped a big fat sponge and smoothed it over her breasts to the place where her baby once had rested. She had buried her future along with her past, the day she'd sent Adam out of her life. At best, she was marking time; at worst....

*Steven deserves better*.

Ah, yes. When it came to an accounting, this was her worst sin: making promises before God to love, honor and cherish a man when she knew she had nothing of true value to give him.

She let the sponge fall into the water with a soft plop and curled up, hugging her arms around her knees. Her hair fell forward, trying without success to shield her from her shame.

Of course she could not marry Steven. It had been out of the question from the first. If she did not love him as she loved Adam, she at least loved him enough not to condemn him to the role of second best and expect him to pretend it was enough. He had the right to a wife who was free to accept and treasure what he had to bring to their relationship without her yearning for what she couldn't have with someone else. Steven deserved to come first.

And she? What did she deserve?

Exactly what she'd got. Nothing but heartache. And the very real possibility of another unplanned pregnancy.

Her culpability lay not in her having made love with one man while she was engaged to marry another, though God knew that was bad enough. Her greatest sin had been the perpetuation of her own self-deceit which, from the moment he'd stepped back into her life, Adam had exposed with the brutal, uncompromising honesty that was his trademark. It was time to shed the role she'd so conscientiously assumed and go back to accepting who she really was: a rebel, perhaps, but at least one true to her most deeply held beliefs. The charade was over.

Wearily, she toweled herself dry and slipped into a fresh nightgown. She would sleep that night, if not with the innocence of a child then at least with the knowledge that, tomorrow, all aspects of the truth would emerge and the painful business of reparation begin.

She went first to Steven, catching him before he left his apartment for the bank. "I hope this isn't too early," she said without preamble when he opened the door, "but I needed to see you as soon as possible."

"Yes," he said quietly, leaning forward to kiss her cheek. "I thought you might. Have you had breakfast?"

"No."

"May I get you something?"

She shook her head. "No, thank you. Steven, I—"

"Coffee, then?" He lifted a half-full carafe from the breakfast bar in his smart, compact kitchen. "I could use a second shot myself."

What she wanted was to say what she had to say, quickly, before she lost her nerve: that she had done him a terrible injustice in letting him assume responsibility for her happiness; that marriage involved a great deal more than the sharing of "for worse" and with her, he would find little to celebrate in the way of "for better."

She could see, though, that her arrival had disturbed his usual imperturbability and that he needed breathing space to regain command of himself. "All right. Cream, please, and no sugar."

He looked at her with gentle reproof. "I know how you take your coffee, my love," he said, filling a mug and pushing it across to her before refilling his own and coming to perch on the stool next to hers at the bar.

"Of course you do," she said. "After all this time, you know just about everything about me."

"Yes, I do," he said, and took a long, deep breath. "Including the fact that you've come here this morning to tell me what I wouldn't let you say yesterday at the chalet." He sighed again and looked at her. "I'm listening now, Georgia."

How he must be hurting! And how typical that he'd shielded her, fighting her battles for her even though he must have known all along he would wind up the loser.

"I cannot marry you, Steven," she said, her voice shaking almost as much as the hands she closed around her coffee mug. "And I am so sorry that I ever let you believe I could."

"You're still in love with Adam."

"Yes."

"Have you told him?"

"No. It wouldn't do any good. He doesn't love me, or, if he does, not enough."

"I had hoped I could be the one to make up for that," Steven said, loosening the knot in his tie, "but that's not how these things work, is it?"

She blinked furiously, trying to dam the tears that rose up in her throat. "I wish they did," she quavered. "Oh, Steven, I wish it could be you. I want so badly to love you the way a bride should love her groom. You make me feel warm and safe, and I am so afraid to be without you."

He pulled out a linen handkerchief and offered it to her. "Isn't that what marriage is all about, Georgia? Leaning on each other?"

"Yes," she sobbed, "but not if it only comes one way."

"I suppose not." He picked up his mug, then put it down again without drinking. "Have you told your family?"

She mopped her eyes. "No," she sniffed. "I felt I owed it to you to come here first."

"When you see your mother, will you apologize to her for me? I'm afraid I misled her badly when I told her not to worry, and that everything would be all right."

"How could you have known it wouldn't be?"

His smile broke her heart. "Oh, my darling Georgia, everyone knew, even you. You just fought accepting the knowledge longer than the rest of us, that's all. But your mother and your sister..." He shrugged and even drummed up a creditable imitation of a laugh. "Why do you think they were so appalled by Adam's reappearance, if not because they recognized it spelled the end of their hopes for you and me?"

"I don't know how I'm going to tell them."

He covered her hand with his. "Would you like me to do it for you?"

"Of course I would," she cried. "I'd like you to shoulder all the problems and relieve me of having to do a damn thing but think about myself. It's the perfect definition of our relationship—your giving, and my taking without once considering the cost to you."

"You know better than anyone that that's what love's all about, Georgia. Why else did you end your engagement to Adam?"

"Because I didn't want him to feel he was being railroaded into marriage when I found I was pregnant."

"Exactly. And perhaps," Steven suggested gently, "he deserves to be made aware of that fact now. It might make all the difference to the way he presently sees things."

It was something she mulled over during the drive across town to her family's home. But if she decided to follow Steven's advice, it would have to wait its turn. Before that, she had to face her parents and her sister—the latter sooner than she'd expected, she realized, recognizing Samantha's car parked next to their mother's in the driveway.

To her vast surprise, neither woman reacted to her news as she'd expected. Natalie reeled a little but, after a moment, wrapped her arms around Georgia and held her close in a show of affection that was as rare as it was warm. "My darling girl," she said quietly. "I had a feeling this would be the outcome."

Astonishingly, Samantha's eyes filled with tears. "Why?" she wailed. "Why do you have to be different and always do things the hard way?"

Misunderstanding, Georgia sighed and said, "I'm sorry, Sammie. I tried to be the sort of person you all want me to be, but I just don't fit the same conservative mold that suits you so well."

"We don't care, as long as you're happy—and you were, with Steven."

"No, dear." Their mother, who'd gone to sit quietly on the sofa in front of the fire, spoke up. "Georgia hasn't been really happy since before Adam went away. She just worked hard to make us happy and that's not quite the same thing."

Georgia sat down next to her. "Mother, I'm sorry. I know I've disappointed you but my conscience—"

"Conscience, my foot!" Tears still sparkling, Samantha glared. "Adam Cabot's at the bottom of all this, isn't he? Why don't you just admit it, Georgia?"

"All right." Georgia raised her hands in resignation. "But not in the way you think, Samantha. I'm not tossing one man aside to take up with another. Adam doesn't even know that I've called off the wedding.''

"It won't make a bit of difference when he does find out," her sister predicted heatedly. "He broke your heart once, Georgia, and he'll do it again."

"You're probably right," Georgia said. "It's a chance I'll have to take. But I've learned something over the last two days, Sammie. I'd rather be miserable over my own broken heart than be responsible for someone else's, which is what eventually would have happened if I'd gone ahead and married Steven.''

Brave words—as long as she didn't have to act on them, and for the next two weeks the busywork entailed in canceling a wedding occupied all her time. But at last there was no excuse for further procrastination. On the third Monday after her return from the mountains, she phoned Adam and asked him to stop by her house sometime.

"Why?" he wanted to know, clearly not thrilled by the invitation. "The last time you saw me, you said you never wanted to set eyes on me again."

"I know, but it's important that I explain certain things. Please, Adam," she said, sensing a refusal.

"Beats me what we have to talk about," he replied offhandedly, "but if it's that important, sure. How's Sunday evening, around eight or so?"

Almost a week before she could unburden her soul? How could she bear to wait that long? "Fine," she said.

She kept herself busy in a flurry of seasonal activity. As usual for the days leading up to Christmas week, business was brisk at the studio. During the evenings, she spent her time cleaning her house from top to bottom, filling the rooms with fresh flowers, stringing dozens of tiny white Christmas lights through the wisteria vine climbing up the wall outside her front door, and laying in a supply of the French Merlot Adam used to enjoy so much.

On the Saturday, she closed the studio at noon and treated herself to the works at the town's most upscale beauty salon—everything from a facial and haircut to a pedicure. On the way home, she passed a boutique that specialized in items costing more than most people spent on a month's rent, and succumbed to the temptation of a pair of midnight-blue velvet lounging pajamas displayed in the window.

By Sunday evening, bathed, perfumed and jittery as a teenager on a blind date, she posted herself at the window overlooking the drive and practised what she would say. All of which was more than a little ridiculous.

What, after all, did she expect of this meeting? That coming clean about her own motivations and feelings would convince Adam to abandon his mistrust of matrimony and snatch at the chance to plant his ring on her finger again, now that Steven's had been conveniently disposed of? Hardly, if their last private exchange had been any indication of how he really felt about her!

Even the setting for this command performance reflected the new Georgia, Adam decided, as the Rolls whispered to stop at her front door. Demure and graceful on the outside, the house was nevertheless built to last; a survivor with a core of inner fortitude, just like its owner.

She opened the door before he could ring the bell. He had a brief impression of rich, soft velvet anchored at her tiny waist with a gold silk-tasseled cord, and immediately averted his eyes before they went on a visual rampage of the rest of her. Safer by far to concentrate on the decor surrounding him.

"Sorry I'm a bit late," he said, blatantly taking stock of his surroundings.

Unlike the spare elegance of her old apartment with its black lacquered furniture and artfully arranged bird-of-paradise flowers, this place displayed a montage of pastels and mellow old wood, the glimmer of brass and the old-fashioned charm of roses and baby's breath.

Slim hand resting on the newel post at the foot of the stairs, she watched him, gauging his reaction. Slim *left* hand, he noticed, and ringless, as he knew it would be, courtesy of his grandmother's impeccable sources.

"Where'd you hear that?" he'd asked with studied indifference, when she'd told him the Chamberlaine-Drake wedding was off.

"At the hairdresser's, darling grandson of mine." Bev's eyes had sparkled with merry malice. "Where else?"

Should he comment on the news now? Offer his condolences? Or had Georgia asked him here to rake him over the coals and lay the blame for yet another aborted wedding at his feet?

Briefly, his glance collided with hers. "What?" he asked irritably, when she remained silent.

She blinked and ran the tip of her tongue over her lips, evoking an outrageous quiver of desire in him. "I beg your pardon?"

"Why the inspection?" He scowled and willed his flesh to more circumspect behavior. "Do I have broccoli stuck between my front teeth, or something?"

She clutched the newel post at the foot of the stairs more firmly. "Broccoli?" she echoed dazedly. "No. Why do you ask?"

"Because you're staring at me as if there's something sadly amiss with the way I look." He brushed his hands down the front of his sweater and shrugged. "Is it the clothes I'm wearing? Not formal enough for the occasion perhaps?"

"You look perfectly..." She did it again, tormented him with the tip of her tongue. "...perfectly fine," she finished on a sigh.

"In that case, why don't you tell me why you asked me to come over?"

"Yes." She hesitated, and he was all set to warn her: *Keep your damned tongue in your mouth where it belongs unless you're looking for trouble,* when she loosened her death grip on the newel post and sort of gave herself a little shake. With a dainty flourish, she waved him toward an archway leading into the living room. "Come and sit down first. May I pour you a glass of wine?"

"No." In front of the fireplace, two love seats faced each other, separated by a coffee table on which sat a large crystal brandy snifter filled with red-berried holly sprigs and white roses. He parked himself smack in the middle of one sofa and spread his arms along its cushioned back, taking up as much space as possible to preclude the possibility of her coming to sit next to him. There was a limit to how much he could take of her particular brand of subtle attack. "What do you want to talk to me about?"

She looked a little taken aback at his brusqueness. "Well, actually, it's rather a long story, but I suppose I should begin with its ending. Steven and I called off the wedding."

"Why are you telling me?"

"Because you're the reason, Adam."

He rolled his eyes. "You told him what happened at the chalet? Georgia—confession might have been good for your soul, but did it once occur to you that it might not have been particularly good for Steven's? That it might, in fact, have caused him needless pain? Or didn't that—?"

"I didn't tell him," she said.

It took a minute for her words to sink in. "What?"

"I didn't tell him. That's not why we decided to end things."

He eyed her narrowly. "*We* decided—or *you*?"

"I did."

"Well, shoot, why not? You've had more practice, after all."

She winced and twisted her fingers nervously. For a while nothing but the muted tick of a grandmother clock in the corner and the crackle of the logs on the fire disturbed the screaming silence. Then, on a rush of breath, she said, "The reason I had to break off my engagement to Steven is that I'm still in love with you, Adam."

He refused to acknowledge the leap his heart gave. Aware that her teal blue gaze was fixed imploringly on him, he spread his left palm face up. "You have the strangest way of showing it, my dear. Let's see, what are some of the sentiments you've expressed since I came back into your life?" He enumerated them, one at a time, on his fingers. "'I wish you'd stayed dead', 'nobody has ever made me cry the way you do', 'drunken sot', 'horse's—'."

"Don't!" A blush of color flooded her face. "Please don't remind me of what I called you. I'm embarrassed enough already."

"Then there's the small matter of your having told me to take a hike in the first place," he continued heartlessly. "Gee, I'm glad you don't hate me, Georgia."

"You felt pressured into asking me to marry you," she shot back. "You'd made it clear from the start of our involvement that you weren't interested in settling down and the way we argued over every little trifle, once you'd put a ring on my finger, seemed to bear out the fact. When I offered you your freedom, you leapt at the chance to take it."

"As I recall," he said, "what you *demanded* was putting our relationship on hold long enough for me to take the Air Force up on its offer of a two month extension of duty so that I could test out their new fighter jet, and you could decide if you were ready to become Mrs. Adam Cabot."

"Remember it any way you please." Agitated, she got up from her seat in a swirl of exotic perfume and dark blue velvet. "I'm going to pour myself a club soda. Are you sure you won't change your mind about the wine?"

When he shook his head, she went on, "The fact remains that when you left so willingly, I knew I'd done the right thing."

"Very decent of you, I'm sure. Your family must have been so proud that you didn't demean yourself by begging me to stay."

"I could have," she said, her voice suddenly tight with anguish. "I could have tried to hold on to you with the best reason in the world."

Premonition laid a cold finger along his spine, cooling the furor her other disclosures had aroused in him. "And what reason is that, Georgia?"

The glass she held rattled against the bottle of club soda in her other hand, a musical tinkling as if a breeze had disturbed a chandelier. "I was pregnant at the time," she said baldly.

"*What*?"

"And I thought," she continued, "that if you came back to me voluntarily, it would be a sign that we really were meant for each other. And if you didn't—" Her voice rose and fell, tossed on a wave of unshed tears.

"—then I didn't want you on any other terms, especially not out of a sense of obligation."

"You withheld from me the fact that you were pregnant, knowing as you did how I feel about children being deserted by their parents? Knowing that I would no more turn my back on a child of mine than I'd—"

"I had only just found out, Adam. It was early days and I thought there'd be plenty of time to tell you, when—*if*—"

"*Where is my baby?*"

She half turned toward him and shook her head. "There is no baby," she whispered.

He lunged up from the love seat, a red haze blurring his vision. "You killed my child?"

Soda water splashed out of the bottle, missing her glass and puddling instead on the silver serving tray. "No! You know me better than to ask such a thing!"

"I don't know you at all," he informed her savagely. "You've proved that over and over again. First, you manufacture a reason to break our engagement, then you decide to withhold the news that you're carrying my child. Then, when it seems you've been cheated out of a grand reconciliation, you glom on to my best friend and make him jump through hoops instead. You aren't the woman I fell in love with, Georgia. You've become a control freak who manipulates people and circumstances to suit her whim."

"Well," she said shakily, "you did say, when we were at the chalet, that you almost hated me. I'm beginning to believe you meant it."

"So am I, Georgia," he said. "So am I."

# CHAPTER EIGHT

HE HURLED the words at her with the deadly accuracy of a bomb finding its mark. The silence in its wake was deafening. Reeling from the shock, Georgia pressed her lips together in an attempt to still their trembling.

He looked as dismayed as she felt. They stared at each other across the width of the room and Georgia knew they'd reached a crisis point. Either she told him all that was in her heart and risked losing him, or she guaranteed it by retreating into that wasteland that had been her emotional shelter for so long.

"I have always loved you," she replied, dredging up the courage to make the admission. "Enough to let you follow your dream then, Adam, and enough to bare my soul to you now."

For the longest time he simply stared at her. Then he passed a weary hand across his eyes and, coming to where she stood at the table, said, "Oh, hell, I can see this is going to turn into a long evening. Maybe I'll have some of that wine, after all."

Caught squarely between dismay and optimism, Georgia nodded and swabbed ineffectually with a paper serviette at the puddle of club soda before reaching for the Merlot. "All right."

"Better let me," Adam said, removing the bottle from her hands, "before you make an even bigger mess of things."

"That does seem to be what I'm best at, doesn't it?" she remarked, with a faltering stab at levity. "Pity it isn't a marketable commodity."

"Go sit down, Georgia," he replied, not ungently pushing her aside. Even in the midst of uncertainty, part of her warmed to his touch. "And stop berating yourself for not living up to your own impossibly high expectations. We all make mistakes but they become unpardonable only if we keep on repeating them."

While she dwelt on the wisdom of that observation, he filled two glasses and placed them on the coffee table, then resumed his seat across from her.

"It seems to me," he said reflectively, "that we somehow have to figure out a way to air our grievances—and there's no denying we harbor more than a few toward one another—with a modicum of respect for each other's feelings. What I said, a moment ago..." He blew out a breath. "...was inexcusable. I'm sorry if I insulted you."

"You ought to have known better than to think I would have aborted our baby."

"And you ought to have told me you were pregnant. It was my baby, too, and I had a right to know."

"I planned to tell you eventually, but not then, not when you were torn between two alternatives. It was more important for you to find out what you really wanted, me or your work."

His lips tightened in annoyance. "It's a real pity that, in deciding what was important, you failed to include the fact that love involves trust. The bottom line, Georgia, is that you didn't love me enough to trust me."

"I loved you enough to give you your freedom," she cried. "Maybe I loved you too much."

"No!" He chopped his hand through the air in denial. "You manipulated our relationship and you're still doing it. You always have to have control, and that's how we arrived at the point we're at now. Not because you loved me too much but because you didn't believe I loved you enough. And having decided that, you thought you'd better take steps to protect yourself, even to the point of depriving me of the knowledge of my baby.''

She bowed her head to hide the despair that she knew was flooding her eyes. ''So what are you saying, Adam? That too much has happened and now it's too late for us?''

''I think a more relevant question might be, is it too soon?'' Heaving a mighty sigh, he swirled his wine moodily. ''You've always claimed to be the rebel in your family, the one that didn't follow the conventional route, but that's not really true. You want the house, mortgage, and two and a half children just as badly as Sammie wants them. You just go about getting them a different way, that's all.''

Surprise had her snapping to attention. ''That's crazy!''

''Is it? When we met, you claimed to be a free spirit, a woman too involved in her work to have the time or inclination for the ties of marriage. Yet—''

''I know—I know!'' Beleaguered by the uncompromising logic of his argument, she slumped against the cushioned arm of the couch and leaned her head against her hand. ''When I met you, all those fine resolutions flew out of the window. That's what love does to a woman, Adam. Takes over her life and redefines its parameters.''

''You call that love?'' There was no mistaking the drawling cynicism in his voice. ''Then how do you explain that when I seemed to be gone permanently, you took up with Steven? Or how, now that I'm back, you're ready to drop him and pick up where we left off? The way I see it, that doesn't spell 'love' so much as 'desperate to get married', Georgia.''

"I already told you, I never loved Steven the way I love you."

"But you were willing to marry him when you thought you couldn't have me, and that brings us to real question of why you asked me over here tonight."

As though he found the atmosphere too stifling, he surged up from the couch and went to stand at the window. Her gaze followed him, recording how well the cranberry sweater and white shirt he wore over dark gray slacks showcased the austere grace of his figure.

Without turning, he suddenly rapped out, "What is it you want now, Georgia? Another proposal from me? Another ring? And if I decide I'm not interested, what then? Will you go running back to Steven and tell him it was all a big mistake, that *he*'s the one you really want?"

She couldn't blame him for his misgivings. All she could do was face them without flinching or attempting to refute them. "*Aren't* you interested?" she asked in a low voice.

Time slowed to the agonized ticking of milliseconds before he condescended to face her again. She saw his brows draw together, his chest rise and fall beneath the cranberry sweater. His irises, normally deeply blue as summer dusk, blazed into smoking passion.

"I wish I weren't," he growled. "And if that's too much to ask, then I wish to God that I could lie as easily as you seem able to do."

Her hopes crumpled in a tinkling heap. "If that's how you see things between us," she said, "then we're no further ahead than we were fifteen months ago. I'll get your coat."

Vision blurred with disappointment, she groped her way to the front hall. Her hands closed over the soft leather of his jacket and it was all she could do not to bury her face in it and howl. But she'd made fool enough of herself for one night; she'd save the hysterics for when he'd gone. Heaven knew, she'd have the rest of her life to bewail having lost him.

"I think you'd better explain that remark," he said from close behind, which was the first indication she had that he'd followed her. Just how close he was, though, didn't become apparent until she spun around and found herself brought up short against his chest.

"I'd have thought it was plain enough," she said, hopelessly enmeshed in the warm, masculine scent of him. "When it comes to our relationship, we both shy away from the truth. The thought of commitment still has you reacting like a man being led to the slaughter, and I'm still afraid of what it will cost me if I let you know how deeply I care for you. One thing, however, *has* changed: I no longer want anything from you unless you're able to offer it without reservation. If I have to grovel to get you to admit you love me, I'd as soon do without."

Even to admit such a thing was pure anguish. Hanging on to her composure by a thread, she tossed the jacket at him. "You see, I do listen to your advice, Adam. I'm not making the same mistake again."

Flinging aside the jacket, he let fly with a shocking obscenity. "You make me crazy, do you know that?" he whispered savagely. "When I'm around you, I don't function up here—" He stabbed a finger at his temple in disgust. "All I want is to strip you naked and lose myself in you, and never mind whose ring is on your finger."

"Yes, well . . ." Her breath jerked raggedly. "That's more or less what happened that night at the chalet and then, once you'd got what you wanted, you told me it meant nothing, that it was just sex. Another big mistake, right?"

"What happened that night at the chalet was too briefly clandestine to qualify as anything other than what it was, an unplanned coupling that didn't begin to satisfy either one of us," he said hoarsely, tracing fiery circles over the palm of her hand with sensuous intent.

"Speak for yourself." She tried to sound coolly unmoved but conviction was hard to project with desire weaving from that one point of contact to suffuse her entire body with heat. "In fact, why don't you take your own advice and stop trying to second-guess—"

He leaned forward and kissed her, taking her by such surprise that she was caught with her mouth open. And once his lips touched hers, she had no desire to close it. Quite the opposite, in fact. She yearned toward him, offering herself so blatantly that he could not possibly have misunderstood the message for anything other than what it was: permission, pure and simple, to have his way with her.

Because he was the most contrary and infuriating man in the world, however, he contented himself—and tortured her—by choosing to sample but not possess. Holding her hands firmly by her side, he kept her at just enough of a distance to prevent her from supporting herself against him, and bent his energies to reducing her to a moaning, writhing mass of submission barely able to keep itself upright.

"I might have known you'd take advantage of me," she moaned softly.

"Rubbish!" Barely lifting his mouth from hers, he swung their joined hands in a wide arc to meet behind her back. "If you want me to stop, all you have to do is tell me. It's your call, Georgia."

How could she make the decision with her body and heart in frightening conspiracy against the rational part of her that warned: This is not the way! First, we must resolve the differences, reestablish the trust, before we give way to passion.

But trust was a vague commodity, not easily identified except by its absence, whereas passion was unmistakable in its clamor for recognition.

She searched avidly for his mouth again, hoping he'd choose to interpret correctly her little whimper of acquiescence and thus spare her having to make the choice, but he would have none of it.

"I'm waiting, Georgia," he said, his voice vibrating deliciously against her lips. "Tell me what you want."

Desire ran too high to be denied. "I want you," she admitted on a defeated sigh. "I want you. Now."

She couldn't know how close he was to flash point. He didn't want to think about it himself. If she had refused him....

But she had not. She had given him permission because the fever that had taken hold of him had reached out to infect her, too. Her blue-green eyes were wide and glazed, her breathing ragged, and if he was hard with arousal, so was she. Not even the rich drape of velvet could disguise the almost visible pulsing of her breasts or their tautly pebbled tips.

The need to touch her, to inhale the fragrance of her skin, to taste it, damn near destroyed him. Reaching out, he tore her tunic loose from its buttoned closure and bared her shoulder. One more swift, sharp tug and she was naked to the waist except for the lacy peach absurdity of her bra.

It was the first time in over a year that he had not looked at her from the fog of dreams and darkness. With an aching fascination, he watched the rise and fall of her breasts, observed his thumbs hook inside the band holding up her wide-legged trousers and eased it past her waist to the sweet slender curve of her hips.

Infected by the same compelling urge, she moved to touch him, her gaze roaming in the wake of her fingers as they trailed down the flat plane of his abdomen to his belt buckle and beyond until, with torturous delicacy, they found his groin.

"Now, Adam," she repeated on a scrap of breath, then, in a gesture so artlessly generous and erotic that he could have wept, sank to her knees and pillowed her cheek against the swollen ridge of his arousal.

The stamina of Hercules would not have been enough to withstand such seduction and Adam was long past the point of pretending he was immortal. With a growl of agonized pleasure, he bent and swept her into his arms. "Not yet, and not here," he muttered against her throat.

Taking the stairs two at a time, he shouldered his way through a half-open door on the left of the landing and found himself in a room awash with subdued lamplight. He retained a blurred impression of rich mahogany, white eyelet cotton, wallpapered pink cabbage roses climbing over a slanting ceiling, but his chief focus was the bed with its pencil-slim posts and fat pillows.

The mattress sighed gently beneath their weight, tolerated with well-sprung long-suffering the stripping away of their clothing, and settled quietly about their bodies as they came together, nesting from chin to toe in perfect alignment.

"*Now*, Adam," she said again, her lips reaching blindly for his and her fingernails digging into the flesh of his shoulders.

"Soon," he assured her, the last rational corner of his mind determining that, this time, reckless haste would not mar the glory.

He didn't know what came after tonight. If what they were about to share marked the end, he intended to preserve in perfect clarity the memory of it. If, on the other hand, it should turn out to denote a new beginning, it would serve as a banner for the rest of their lives. "Let me hold you first... let me get to know you again."

Memory had not deceived him, except in his perceptions of how long he could withstand the temptation of her. She was as delicately fashioned as ever, at once reed slender and softly feminine. If he could bottle the fragrance of her, he'd be a millionaire overnight, he thought hazily, burying his lips in her hair. He wanted to kiss her for hours, investigate at leisure the exquisite texture of her skin, feast indefinitely on the rosy tip of her breast.

He might have succeeded in all three had she been content to accept his homage but she was a fiend disguised as an angel, tormenting him with *her* mouth, *her* hands, *her* lips. When, in retaliation, he slid his tongue the length of her and tasted her milky sweetness, time became not an ally but a foe.

Sensation rippled through Georgia, fiery, intoxicating. Quivering with sudden shock, she arched above him, crying out his name with a lost hopelessness. "... Please," she begged. "Adam, please..."

She heard the pleading and didn't care that, only minutes before, she'd sworn she'd never beg him for anything, ever again. What did such a promise matter compared to the imperative demands of the heart or the silent call of the soul?

He touched her again, delicately, deliberately, tormenting her with pleasure. The tide within gathered speed, and she was as helpless to stop it as she was to hide it. He had to know he had her at his mercy and that, if retribution reigned uppermost in his mind, now was the time to punish her. All he had to do was push away from the bed and leave the indifferent touch of night to cool the fever running through her blood.

There was nothing uncertain about his intention, though, nor, unlike that night at the chalet, anything drowsy or dreamlike about his loving. Everything, from the merest whisper of his lips over her skin to the liquid throb of desire invoked by his clever hands, forged itself in her memory in acute and vibrant detail.

Blindly, she reached for him, urging him to come to her fully, to end the aching void and fill her with his vitality and warmth.

"I never wanted any other man, Adam...only you..." she whispered raggedly, imprinting the shape and texture of him on her fingertips.

She should have remained quiet. Should have contented herself by showing him, instead of trying to convey something that reached too far beyond the scope of words to serve any other purpose than remind him that she *had* tried, however unsuccessfully, to turn to Steven.

Bracing himself with a hand on each side of her head, Adam raised himself to arm's length and stared down at her. In the softly shadowed room, his eyes were haunted and she understood fully, perhaps for the first time, how much she had hurt him by her defection.

"No!" She touched his mouth with trembling fingers to still the accusation before he could voice it aloud. "We were never lovers."

She felt rather than saw the doubt flicker through him and knew that if she didn't convince him now, there would never come another time. Trapping him in her gaze, she slid the palms of her hands rapidly past the corrugated symmetry of his belly. Flagrant and unashamed, she incited him to new fire. "If it can't be you, Adam," she vowed huskily, "it will never be anyone. I know that, now."

She heard his strangled moan of pleasure, saw the blue of his eyes turn sultry with contained passion. Quickly, before he had time to consider the wisdom of succumbing to the temptation she offered, she strained against him, cupped her palms over his buttocks and tugged him down to meet her willing flesh.

He groaned softly, cursing himself and her, and claimed her. Blindly and utterly, pressing her into the mattress and moving within her with the frenzied discipline of a man striving not to be pushed too quickly beyond the limits of his endurance.

He filled an emptiness in her that went beyond the gratification of the moment. He buried his mouth at her ear, found its most sensitive spot, and with his tongue delivered a string of tiny raptures that threaded to her breasts and ended in a knot of tension low in her womb. As the rhythm of his loving took hold, all the sensual awareness which had slumbered through most of the last fifteen months exploded into life. The first distant spasms of completion quivered down her spine.

She tried to delay it, to savor the moment. To deploy all her senses in the preservation of it. But Adam drove her hard, racing his own heart to the finish and sweeping hers along with it. The explosion, when it came, shattered the silence and rocketed them both beyond time or place. All she could do was cling fiercely to him and accept that neither of them retained control. In the throes of such raging splendor, passion ruled the moment.

*    *    *

The night stole back softly, leaving her with the languid perception of having survived a sort of holocaust. That, in its wake, she and Adam found themselves still meshed together, their limbs entwined and their bodies outwardly intact, struck Georgia as ludicrous. They should have been shattered into a thousand parts and flung beyond the pull of earth's gravity.

Beneath her breast, her heartbeat stabilized. She felt again the fine cotton sheet at her back, saw the cabbage roses still climbing merrily over the ceiling, heard the distant hoot of an owl. For just a very short time, she felt completely happy. Until Adam stirred.

He lifted his head and subjected her to a long and thorough scrutiny. She waited for him to speak, to put an end to the silence unspooling around them, but he said nothing. Instead, he rolled away from her and swung his legs over the side of the bed.

She laid a tentative hand in the small of his back. "Adam?"

He didn't so much flinch away from her as withdraw into himself. The way he did it, with an infinitesimal shrug that barely caused a ripple beneath her hand, left her feeling as though she'd committed a dreadful breach of good manners to have dared touch him in the first place.

He leaned forward, his spine flexing long and elegant in the lamplight, and reached for his clothes. Only after he'd buckled the belt to his slacks and was shrugging into his shirt did he speak.

"Well," he said, deftly slipping buttons into place, "what next?"

"Next?" Intimidated by his tone and the absolute inscrutability of his expression, she touched the tip of her tongue to her lips nervously. "I'm not sure what you mean."

"What do you expect of me, Georgia? What am I supposed to do or say now?"

"Whatever you want to say or do." She lifted her shoulders sadly. "You're not under any sort of obligation, Adam."

He tugged his sweater over his head. "That's good," he said, finger-combing his hair into place. "Because I might as well tell you right now that I won't let you use what happened tonight as a weapon."

"To do what?"

"Coerce me into reciting things you want to hear that I'm not ready to say."

She sprang up, clutching the sheet beneath her chin. Spots of anger burned holes in her cheeks. "I would never do that, and that you would think, even for a minute, that I would, tells me that you were right earlier when you said that you don't know me at all."

"No, I don't," he said wearily, turning away from her. "What's worse, I don't know myself, either. The future isn't staring me in the face, all neatly laid out and waiting to be picked up where the past left off. I'm not the same man I was and you sure as hell aren't the same woman. In some ways, we're strangers in familiar bodies."

She'd known that physical loving alone wouldn't be enough to wipe away the hurt or restore them to what they'd once been to each other. But even so, *strangers*? "You're wrong, Adam," she said, watching him. "Strangers don't connect the way we did tonight."

He paced to the door, his shoulders cutting a rigid angle from his neck, his stance parade-ground perfect. "Sure they do," he said, ramming his hands into his hip pockets so violently that the fabric threatened to rip away from his slacks. "All the time. Only fools pretend it has lasting significance."

"I do not believe," Georgia said slowly, "that two people can share our sort of..." She reached her fingers in the air and spread them wide, searching for exactly the term. "...intense harmony of body and heart, unless there is something deeper involved than mere—" She stopped again, groping for words.

"Lust?" he supplied, tossing the word over his shoulder.

"No," she cried, looping the sheet beneath her arms and holding it in front of her as she scrambled from the bed and went to stand next to him. It was, she supposed, a rather ridiculous gesture of modesty, coming at that particular time, but the pain of what he was saying was hard enough to bear. She didn't think she could endure his scornful gaze raking over her, as well. "It meant much more than that to me, Adam, and I believe it was more than just—" She swallowed. "—a roll in the hay for you, too."

She didn't know quite how she expected him to respond to that. Surprisingly, he chuckled, and if the sound wasn't entirely without reserve, it at least lacked the satirical ring that had marked his laughter of late. "No," he agreed, his eyes dancing with sapphire amusement. "No, I don't think that's what I'd call it, either."

"Thank you for that much," she said.

Sobering, he touched the underside of her jaw with gentle fingers. "Right now, it would be very easy for me to tell you that I love you."

"I wish you would," she whispered, her eyes suddenly brimming over. "Because, Adam, I love you, I truly do. More than I ever guessed."

With the ball of his thumb, he diverted her tears. "I once thought love was all it took, sweet pea. Now, I'm not sure it's enough."

Hearts had no business shattering so silently. At the very least, there ought to have been the faint chime of crystal smashing to small pieces. She pressed her lips tightly together as the tears threatened again. Drawing the sheet and her dignity around her like a shroud, she tipped her head in mute defeat and pushed her way past him.

Once inside the bathroom, she locked the door and ran the shower full-force. The water scoured her pitilessly but she scarcely noticed. What mattered was that it drowned out the sound of her sobbing and that she stayed under its pulsing spray long enough to give Adam time to make a tactful exit. She did not want to face him again. She could not.

When she finally turned off the taps, the silence of the house closed around her so completely that she knew he had gone. Automatically, she dried and powdered her body, combed the tangles out of her hair, smoothed night cream over her face and neck. Then, with only her mouth slightly swollen from his lovemaking and the puffiness around her eyes testament to its unhappy aftermath, she went down to lock the front door.

Her blue velvet pajama suit hung tidily over the newel post at the foot of the stairs. *Abandoned like me*, she thought, and was in the process of securing the dead bolt when his voice floated out from just beyond the living room arch and halted her.

"I was just about to come up and see if you'd drowned," he said, moving forward and casting a long shadow over the wall beside her.

# CHAPTER NINE

"AND I thought you'd gone," she said, in the same sort of uppity tone her sister, Samantha, was wont to use on bad waiters. If he hadn't known Georgia better, Adam would have withered at the chill displeasure she emitted. But although she tried to appear calm, he noticed the tremor of her hand as she fumbled with the lock.

"Before we've finished our conversation?" He reached over her shoulder and clicked the dead bolt into place for her. "That would have defeated the whole purpose of my coming here tonight, wouldn't it?"

She turned her head the other way. "I can't imagine that there's anything left to say."

"Perhaps not by you, but there are a few things I'd like to explain."

"Please don't," she said, unlocking the door again with an exaggerated snap. "I've heard enough for one night. For the rest of my life, come to that. If you wanted to spoil my romantic ideals, it should make you happy to hear that you succeeded. I will never again make the mistake of thinking love can overcome any obstacle. Now, please go."

"No." He shoved the dead bolt into its sleeve a second time and spun her around to confront him.

"Don't!" she snapped, pushing at her wet hair. "I look like hell."

"Yes, you do," he conceded. "Isn't it nice that we finally agree on something?"

At that, her lower lip pouted deliciously and he had to remind himself that the reason he'd waited for her to come out of the bathroom had nothing to do with wanting to kiss her and everything to do with making her understand what had prompted him to utter those destructive words upstairs.

"You're no oil painting yourself," she said waspishly, just the way the old Georgia would have when she was ticked off with him about something. "You look as if you've been put through a meat grinder."

He grinned, seizing the chance to lighten the atmosphere a little. "Rolling around with a sex fiend tends to have that effect on a man," he teased, expecting that she'd lash out at him with another cutting rejoinder.

To his horror, she burst into a fresh bout of tears instead.

"Hey, sweet pea . . .!" Abashed, he caught her loosely in his arms. "Stop this, please! I was joking. For a minute, I forgot that you're not as hard-boiled as you used to be."

"I never was," she wailed, wiping her streaming eyes on his shirt. "I pretended to be, because that's what I thought you wanted."

"Maybe that's where we went wrong, then—both of us pretending, just to keep the other one happy. Relationships can't survive on that sort of foundation."

She sniffed. "Exactly. So, since we're mutually agreed we're better off without each other, why are you still hanging around?"

"Because I want to tell you about my recent past. Perhaps then you'll understand why the immediate future isn't as clear to me as you claim it is to you."

"I already understand." She pushed away from him and trailed down the hall to the kitchen. "I got the message loud and clear that you no longer want me in your life. There's no need to repeat it."

"I cannot marry you at this time, Georgia," he said, following her, "because I am not free to offer you the absolute commitment that I know you want, and half measures create nothing but uncertainty and misery. That sort of thing is corrosive. It eats at a relationship, if not sooner, then certainly later as we both well know, and a wedding ring simply isn't talisman enough to prevent it. Which is why I said that love isn't enough."

"Being with you is all I need to make me happy," she said stubbornly, filling a white enameled teakettle and setting it on the stove.

"Is it?" He swept an arm around the room. "Even if I told you I wanted to go back to the Arctic, to a place where the closest thing to a designer kitchen is an oil stove and a year-round refrigerator courtesy of nature? Where the only long-distance transportation is a sled pulled by a team of huskies, and long winter underwear is a staple item of ladies' lingerie?"

As he'd expected, he caught her attention with that. She swung around incredulously. "Are you seriously asking me to believe that you want to go back and live in the Arctic?"

"I have to go back there," he amended, but she either missed the fine distinction or chose to ignore it.

"*Why*?" The question emerged as a wail of dismay.

"Because I have a debt to pay and that's what I wanted to explain to you. Now are you ready to listen?"

He took it as assent when she reached for a japanned canister and said, "I'm making tea. Do you want a cup?"

"Sure."

"You won't like it," she declared perversely. "It's the herbal kind that you always said tasted like perfume."

*You aren't going to like hearing what I'm about to tell you, either*, he thought grimly. "I'll put up with it, just this once."

She indicated a small round table in the bay window at the other end of the kitchen. "You might as well sit over there, then."

He waited until she'd poured the tea into china mugs and was seated across from him before he began. "I spent most of the last fifteen months learning the language and life-style of a group of people who, by choice, have decided to reject the corrupting influences of the nineties and return to the ways of their forefathers."

"I know. You already told me, you were picked up by a tribe of nomadic hunters somewhere in the Arctic, and couldn't get to a phone."

"Which you clearly don't believe."

"Can you blame me?" she inquired, with a lofty arch of her brows. "Everyone has access to some sort of telecommunication these days, even Santa Claus."

"Not everyone, Georgia. The people who found me spend most of their time in a remote area thousands of miles from civilization as you and I understand it. In order to survive, they move from one site to another, battling a winter so endless and vicious that I don't know how they find the guts to face each new day. The men take terrible risks to keep their families fed, and the women—"

He closed his eyes and as though they'd been waiting to attack, the images filled his mind, unforgivingly stark. A bride's stoic acceptance of her young husband's death from exposure during a blizzard; a grandmother's vigil as a newborn struggled to survive a premature birth; and most of all, Ateka's silent, ongoing grief as she watched Ikut sink into despair after the polar bear attack. Yet not once had they allowed their personal troubles to interfere with their care for the man they'd found half frozen to death on the ice.

"The women," he said with difficulty, "manage to create a feeling of home despite the deprivations and hardships. No television, no hospitals, no schools— nothing but stamina, native lore handed down from one generation to the next, and an abiding belief in the importance of the family unit that we, in our pursuit of other goals, have somehow lost."

"Just like in the movies," Georgia said snippily. "How quaint!"

"Let me assure you, there is nothing the least bit 'Hollywood' about the daily grind of their existence," he snapped, ready to shake her for her refusal to accept the truth of what he was telling her. "Sneer all you like but they revere life and thank God they do, or I'd be dead. For all that survival's such a struggle, when I gate-crashed into their world they put their own concerns aside and took the time to care for me as if my recovery were the most crucial thing on earth."

He stretched his legs and massaged the chronic ache in his left thigh. "I won't bore you with the details. They're not important and you're obviously not interested in hearing them. It's enough to say that packing along a fully grown man too helpless for months to feed himself, or pull his weight in the ongoing battle for survival, was a burden they didn't need."

"I'm grateful to them," Georgia cried. "And I'm trying to understand, I really am. But if you were such a burden, why didn't you leave as soon as you could, instead of staying on with them and causing even more disruption in their lives? What was it that kept you from coming back to me sooner, Adam?"

"By the time my injuries were on the mend, it was May. They had moved further north, to their summer camp, and travel isn't as easy as it is in the winter. They had more important things to take care of during the daylight hours than shipping one man back to civilization and by then I was well enough to be able to help a little. Besides, what did I have to rush home to? You'd told me in no uncertain terms to take a hike."

"Fair enough." Her big, beautiful eyes pleaded with him. "But it sounds like the vacation spot from hell, so why do you want to return?"

"Because there is someone I left behind that I must go back and find."

*There is someone I left behind....*

At last, the truth about what had kept him away so long!

Georgia sucked in a gasp of air. Hadn't she wondered, more than once since his return, if, in the end, it would all come down to this? He had been gone over a year, been embraced by a community in which the women stayed home while the men, in ancient, time-honored fashion, went out to hunt—all the men, that was, except the handsome, blue-eyed stranger.

She tucked clenched fists out of sight under the table and fought to gain control of her breathing which had grown painfully shallow.

Oblivious of the absolute devastation he'd wrought, Adam took a draught of the tea, grimaced at its exotic hibiscus flavor, and blithely elaborated on his statement. "We grew very close, Georgia. During the summer, the days are so long—Land of the Midnight Sun and all that, you know—and the men were sometimes gone for weeks at a time. We—"

"Oh, please!" Stumbling to her feet, she put the length of the kitchen between him and her and wished it could have been an entire continent. "You don't have to draw me a picture. I understand perfectly why it was so difficult for you to tear yourself away and why you must go back."

"Do you?" he said without inflection.

"Yes." She swiped at the mist of tears that persisted in clouding her vision. "What amazes me is that you had the gall to castigate me for turning to Steven when I thought I'd lost you. Yet during all those months that I struggled—"

A sob sheared her voice distastefully high. She heard and didn't care. "—*struggled*, Adam, with the guilt of believing I'd sent you to your death, you were making time with someone else. And you have the bloody nerve to say I never gave you proper credit for having loved me at least as much as I loved you!"

"Are you quite done?" he asked levelly.

"Oh, yes," she said, the tears racing down her face. "And I thank God it's finally over! Perhaps now I can get on with the business of healing, too, because you're not the only one who suffered, Adam, not by a long shot."

"Will it make understanding any easier if I—?"

"Nothing about our relationship has ever been easy!"

"—tell you that the person I'm going back for is a sixteen-year-old boy who lost a leg last year as the result of a polar bear attack?"

In contrast to her heated outburst, Adam delivered the information with damning courtesy. It took her fully half a minute to absorb its impact. Finally, she echoed thinly, "Sixteen-year-old boy?"

"I should think 'lost a leg' might be the more relevant phrase, Georgia," he chided.

"Yes," she said, shame washing aside hurt in a mortifying blush. "Of course it is. How awful for him! I'm so sorry that I... jumped to the wrong conclusion."

She stole a glance at him. He remained still seated at the table, his handsome, beloved face inexpressibly sad. "I'm sorry you have so little faith in me," he said.

She felt like a child who'd been entrusted with some priceless treasure, then carelessly smashed it. "I love you," she whispered hopelessly, her face crumpling.

"And I love you. But without the trust to go with it, the love doesn't stand a chance, Georgia."

She heard him push back the chair, heard his tread on the floor, and knew with dull certainty that nothing short of a miracle would prevent him from walking out of her front door and out of her life, this time for good.

She flung herself after him. "Adam, please don't go," she cried, catching up with him in the hall where he'd stopped to put on his jacket. "I know I said I wouldn't grovel for your love, but I'm begging you, please, don't do this to us, not now, just when we've been given a second chance."

He bathed her in a sorrowful glance. "You're the one with the destructive bent, not I," he said wearily. "Do you know that the one thing that kept me going when things were at their worst was the thought that, if only I could be reunited with you, I wouldn't make the same mistakes again? I promised myself there'd be no more wanting the moon, no more separations, no more infantile bickering over things that didn't matter; just you and me making a life together, and to hell with all the rest."

He jerked the zipper of his jacket closed and snapped the studs at his cuffs. "Thanks to the Inuit, I did more than recover from my injuries, I grew up, too—a bit late by most people's standards, I guess. Went away with part of me still a kid yearning for adventure, and came home a man who'd finally got his priorities in order. It hasn't done us much good, has it?"

"Because it was different for you, don't you see that?" She *was* groveling and didn't care. If she had to prostrate herself to get him to listen, she would. "All during that time, you knew a future together was still possible for us. Eventually, you could come home to me. But I didn't have that to cling to. I had nothing—not even your baby." She started to cry again. "I spent over a year learning to live with your death. I stopped expecting miracles, Adam. I stopped believing in happiness."

"And my coming back did nothing to restore that belief," he said flatly. "Face it, Georgia! We've done a spectacular job of perpetuating our misery when we should have been reinforcing our bonds."

He had his hand on the door. In horrible slow motion, she watched his long, graceful fingers close around the knob and turn it. It felt as if he were draining the lifeblood out of her.

"No," she wept, wrapping her arms around his waist and hanging on for dear life. "Don't you dare walk out on me! I won't lose you again!"

He felt like granite to the touch. Hard, cold, indifferent. "What if I refuse to stay?"

Desperation made her crazy. "I'll follow you," she promised rashly. "I don't care where you go, I'll be right behind you."

"And what if I told you the only way you can convince me that we might have a future together is to let me go again, for however long it might take, with no promises and no guarantees between us except that I will continue to love you just as I always have?"

The questions hammered inside her head. *Why do you have to go? What can you possibly hope to accomplish? How will you find a small band of nomadic hunters in the vast and empty wilderness of the Arctic?* But she knew that to ask them was to destroy the last tenuous hope of their ever finding their way back to each other.

"I would do it," she whispered, quickly, before she lost her courage. "I would do it in a heartbeat."

"Even if it meant having no contact with me for weeks, possibly even months?"

"Even then."

"Finding Ikut is one thing, you know; convincing him to leave his band and move maybe thousands of miles away is another. I'm not likely to accomplish it overnight. And when I succeed—because believe me, Georgia, I do not intend to come back until I have—I'll make sure he's adjusted and settled into his new environment before I abandon him. This is one life that isn't going down the tubes for lack of opportunity, I promise you."

"I understand. I won't ask you to leave the job half done and I'll be waiting for you, however long it takes."

He turned back to her then and she saw that his eyes were suspiciously bright. "When did you become such a devil for punishment, sweet pea?" he murmured hoarsely, taking her into his arms.

"The day I met you," she whispered against his mouth.

They talked far into the night but, more important, they listened to each other and in doing so let down many of the barriers behind which they'd tried to protect themselves.

"I never really confronted fear," Adam confided, "until I felt that fighter jet start buffeting around me during the test flight. Then, all of a sudden, with death staring me in the face, I found myself wondering what the hell I was trying to prove."

"I never really faced up to living without you," Georgia confessed. "Instead, I retired into a sort of limbo where nothing could really touch me. I drifted through the days and would probably..." She cast a nervous glance at him, loath to bring up a subject that might cause another rift between them but knowing that they could make a new start only when all the skeletons had been dragged out of the closet. "...have drifted into marriage with Steven if you hadn't come back when you did. He mourned you almost as much as I did, Adam. He really is your friend."

"Yeah." Adam shrugged. "I know. I guess I knew the night he told me where I could find you, then stood aside and gave me a clear shot at trying to win you back again. Did he know about the baby?"

"Yes. He was the only one who did."

"If you hadn't miscarried, would you still have agreed to marry him?"

"I don't know. Perhaps, if I'd had the baby, I wouldn't have needed anyone else. Your child would have been enough. But let's not talk about what might have been." Or what, God help her, she suspected might be to come. Her period was only a few days late; it was much too soon to be certain that she had become pregnant that night at the chalet—and, once again, much too late to share her suspicions with Adam.

She drew him down to the rug in front of the fire. "Tell me about the boy you want to find," she said. "What is it you want to do for him?"

"Give him hope for the future. He was the pride of his community before the accident—good-looking, bright, a skilled hunter, a natural leader."

"But surely, if his people valued the life of a stranger, they wouldn't turn away from one of their own?"

"No, never." He pulled her head into the crook of his shoulder and combed his fingers absently through her hair. "He's the one turning away from them because he feels useless. The body is incomplete and while, in our culture, we might not view that as calamitous, for him it spells disaster. The future stretches in front of him, empty of all the standards by which a whole man is measured. He sees himself as a long-term burden and I'm afraid that, sooner or later, despair will get the better of him. He'll haul himself outside one day and just disappear into the snow, unless he finds another way to give of himself."

"Will a prosthesis help him, do you think?"

"It might, to some extent. But even if it doesn't—*especially* if it doesn't—I want to give him the chance to broaden his options and realize other ways of leaving his mark. He's got a fine mind, Georgia. There are things he could learn—technology, medicine... Hell, I don't have the final answer; I don't even know for sure there *is* an answer! All I am certain of is that he deserves another shot at life every bit as much as I did, and I intend to see he gets it."

"He'll need money."

"I've got money. Plenty of it."

"And emotional support."

"Yes." His hand slid to her chin and tilted her face to his. "This won't be a one-shot effort. I'll be involved with him for a long time, maybe for the rest of my life."

And this was the man she'd once labeled selfish and uncaring? "It's no wonder I can't help loving you, Adam Cabot."

"If you and I eventually do get married—"

"I'll be involved, too," she assured him. "I already am. Where do you plan to take him?"

"Not to Vancouver or any city like that. The culture shock would be too much, coming on top of everything else he's gone through, but there are good facilities up north that aren't such a long jump from home. I'll look into all that later. Right now, I'm more concerned with finding him before it's too late. The long, dark days of winter encourage depression and I don't know if he'll hold out until the Spring."

He'd given her the perfect lead-in for the one question she'd tried to avoid. "When do you have to go?"

"In the morning," he said. "My leave's up tomorrow night and that's when I have to check in with my C.O. since, technically, I still belong to the Air Force. I was AWOL for over a year, remember, but my debriefing is complete and I expect to be a free agent within a couple of weeks. As soon as that happens, I'll get started."

She closed her eyes and prayed for the courage to deal with the rest. "And how," she asked carefully, "will you go about finding Ikut, once you're a civilian again?"

"Fly the first leg of the journey. I've got a pretty good idea of the circuit the band follows and know where to start looking."

Oh, God, it was a variation of the same nightmare that had taken him away from her before! "Alone?"

He heard the tremor in her voice that she tried so hard to conceal. "I'm not planning to crash-land on the nearest ice floe and just start hiking, sweet pea," he said, a smile curling over his words. "I'll go in the same way I came out. There's an air field used by men on the oil rigs that serves as a supply base for the Inuit hunters, too. I'll pick up a guide and start from there. Don't worry, I won't come back in a body bag. Besides, haven't I already proved that only the good die young?"

She was grasping at straws, she knew, but she couldn't help herself. "But the days are so short. Wouldn't it be easier to wait until the summer?"

"No. I already told you, travel's more difficult then. And if I leave it any longer, I could be too late—if I'm not already." He sighed. "Are you having second thoughts, Georgia? Am I asking for more than you can give?"

"No," she said, knowing in her heart that his way was the only way. If she reneged on her promise now, their future would be forever flawed. There'd always be that niggling doubt in his mind that she didn't trust him enough, and the awful fear in hers that, one day, he'd put them both to the test again.

Just as the sky to the east showed a sliver of light, they made love for the last time. Slowly and exquisitely.

Shortly after, he kissed her goodbye. Kissed her with such ineffable tenderness and regret that the river of fear started flowing again.

*Don't go*, her heart cried out. *Don't endanger our love again.*

But because she knew that only by letting him go could she find out for sure if he would come back to her, she clung to him for one long, last moment then pushed him out of the door.

"Go," she said. "Do what you have to do and know that I love you for it."

Before climbing into the Rolls, he stopped and gave her the thumbs-up sign, the way he always had before when his furlough was up and it was time to leave her again. "I'll be seeing you," he called softly. "Trust me."

She nodded and waved and smiled brightly. "Safe journey, my darling," she replied, closed the door, and before he'd driven as far as the end of her driveway, burst into the worst bout of tears yet, a cleansing torrent that she indulged until she was too exhausted to cry another drop.

Then she washed her face, dressed, and drove to the nearest pharmacy where she bought a home pregnancy kit. It didn't take long, once she got home again, to find the answer she sought.

At half past nine, just about the time that Adam was flying out of Piper Landing on the first leg of his journey back north, she sat down to a solitary breakfast, determined to get on with the business of living.

It wasn't going to be easy, knowing she was pregnant again and not knowing how long it would be before she could tell him. But one thing she was sure about: she wasn't going to be robbed a second time. Not of Adam, and not of his child. Not if she had any say in the matter.

# CHAPTER TEN

ALL THINGS considered, Georgia coped remarkably well in the weeks that followed. She ran the studio, worked in her garden when the weather allowed, turned the smallest bedroom into a nursery when it didn't, and generally managed to present a calm, unruffled face to the world. All this despite the fact that she was plagued with morning sickness and hadn't heard a word from Adam since the phone call he made the day before he'd left with his guide to find the Inuit camp.

So it struck her as nothing short of a stroke of undeserved and vicious bad luck when, just as she was leaving her doctor's office after her twelve week checkup in the second week of February, she collided with her sister right outside the medical clinic.

"What are you doing here?" Samantha wanted to know. "Are you ill?"

"No," Georgia said. "Not exactly."

"Well, you look it." Samantha eyed her critically. "I don't know why you wear beige, Georgia. With your fair coloring, it makes you look faded and anemic."

"Thank you," Georgia said, her stomach rolling unpleasantly. "I needed to hear that, Sammie. What are you doing here?"

Samantha looked coy. "I'll tell you, but you must promise to keep it under your hat because Charles and I haven't told anyone else but our parents. I'm going to have a baby."

Georgia thought she might be sick, right there on the sidewalk. Not because she wasn't glad for her sister but because it bore home to her just how much she wished that she, too, had a husband with whom to celebrate the news. "Congratulations," she said weakly. "When is the baby due?"

"Not until late September." Samantha patted her trim waistline. "I'm only about six weeks along."

By late September, Adam's baby would be over a month old. Would they be a family by then? Would he be by her side for the birth?

"It's good news, Georgia. Charles and I both want this child." Samantha was regarding her curiously. "Look, I'm sorry if you're feeling left out at being the last in the family to hear, but you've been a bit of a stranger with us ever since you broke up with Steven. Mother says she's hardly seen you in months."

"I know. I've been meaning to call or stop by but I've been..." *Throwing up a lot.* "...busy."

Samantha laid an unusually affectionate hand on her arm. "You look about ready to burst into tears. Are you sure you're all right?"

"Yes," Georgia said. "I'm really very happy for you, Sammie. It's just that..."

She stopped, unable to go on as a wave of utter loneliness swept over her. For a minute or two, all those vague half promises Adam had made, all her fierce belief that, before long, he'd come back and they'd be together again, seemed a very flimsy basis on which to build dreams of the future.

"What?"

Was it impending motherhood that lent Samantha a more sympathetic edge, or simply that pregnancy had Georgia's emotions running closer to the surface than usual? Whatever the reason, her chin wobbled alarmingly and she was actually debating the wisdom of telling her sister the whole sorry story when the decision was taken out of her hands.

Maureen Bailey's curly red head popped around the clinic door. "Oh, good, I was hoping I'd catch you before you left, Georgia," the nurse-receptionist chirped. "I forgot to make your ultrasound appointment. It's standard procedure for all new moms these days. Just a precaution, you understand—nothing for you to worry about. If you've got the time, I can take care of it now."

Georgia would have been quite happy if the earth had opened and swallowed her whole. Aware of Samantha at her side, slack-jawed with shock and bristling with outrage, she said faintly, "Actually, Maureen, I'm in a bit of a rush. Why don't you give me a call once you've got it all set up?"

"Sure thing. Oh, hi, Samantha!" Maureen waggled her fingers gaily. "Guess the folks are going to be inundated with grandchildren all at once, eh?"

"Apparently," Samantha croaked, snaking out a hand to halt Georgia as she sidled toward the parking lot. "Georgia, where do you think you're going?"

"To the studio," Georgia replied. "I—"

"Have you told our parents?"

Georgia shrugged and tried to look nonchalant. "Not yet. I thought I still had plenty of time. But now that you know, I suppose it won't remain a secret much longer."

"You suppose right," Samantha said darkly.

"I'll tell them in my own time, Sammie."

"Hah! And when will that be? When it's so obvious to everyone else around town that a person would have to be blind not to notice?"

After that remark, it really shouldn't have come as much of a surprise to Georgia when the bell rang shortly after eight o'clock that night and she opened her front door to find the entire family lined up outside: mother and father, Samantha and Charles, their expressions ranging from grave to scandalized.

They scarcely waited to observe the social amenities before the reproaches and questions began. "Samantha told us your news," her father said. "Why didn't you come to us yourself, Georgia? You can't go through something like this alone and while we don't exactly condone your situation, we're prepared to stand by you. We are your parents, after all."

"I wasn't ready to confide in anyone yet, not even you," Georgia said. "Samantha had no business poking her nose into my affairs."

"I don't suppose it's Steven's?" her mother asked, collapsing with a heartfelt sigh on one of the love seats in the living room.

"Of course it isn't," Samantha scoffed. "If it were, my sister would be a respectably married woman by now. It's that Adam Cabot's baby, isn't it, Georgia?"

"Yes," Georgia said. "May I offer anyone a drink?"

"No," Samantha replied, seemingly having appointed herself family spokesperson. "Instead, you may explain to us, if you can, why that man isn't here now, offering to make an honest woman out of you."

"He's out of town."

Samantha rolled her eyes knowingly. "I bet he is. Miles out of town, probably, as far away as he can get."

"Yes," Georgia said again, more than a little peeved by her sister's attributing the worst possible motives to Adam's absence. "Somewhere in the Arctic, if you really want to know."

"Somewhere in the Arctic?" Georgia's brother-in-law, Charles, spoke up for the first time, preempting Samantha's role of grand inquisitor. "I don't think we like the sound of that. Exactly *where* in the Arctic, Georgia?"

"I don't know," Georgia said.

"When is he coming back?" Her mother and father spoke in worried unison.

"I don't know," she said again.

Charles went to stand with his back to the fireplace. Clasping his soft, white hands behind him, he cleared his throat and pursed his lips into a ludicrous little rosebud. "Do you care, Georgia?" he inquired pompously. "Or doesn't it matter to you one whit that your family is distraught over your latest...error of judgment?"

"Believe it or not, Charles," she informed him tartly, "how the outcome might affect the rest of my family wasn't uppermost in my thoughts at the time conception occurred. And I no more consider my baby an error of judgment than you do yours."

"It's no good appealing to her finer senses, Charles," Samantha said petulantly. "She doesn't have any where Adam Cabot is concerned and never has, since the day she first set eyes on him. One has to wonder what it is about the Lieutenant Colonel that she finds so fatally attractive, especially since his most outstanding talent appears to be his willingness to walk out on her at the drop of a hat—in addition to his knack for making our family the target of gossip all over town."

"Don't upset yourself, Samantha, my love," Charles replied soothingly. "Stress isn't good for you or our infant." He flung Georgia an accusing glare. "As for you, young woman, it's just as well your lover isn't here now because if he were, I'm afraid I'd have to take him outside and teach him a lesson."

Georgia had never been particularly fond of her brother-in-law but, for the sake of peace in the family, she had always been polite to him. This last remark, however, struck her as so absurd that she couldn't help herself. She burst into gales of laughter. "Don't talk like a fool, Charles," she choked. "You'd wind up in a body cast."

"I'm afraid you're the fool, my dear," he replied unctuously, "building your hopes like this. Adam Cabot won't be back and you'll end up with nothing but regrets for the fine opportunity you let pass by the day you sent Steven Drake away. And in the meantime, your whole family is paying the price. I fail to see how you can be so insensitive to their concerns."

"And I fail to understand how the news of one daughter's pregnancy is cause for celebration while news of the other's is treated with all the repugnance of the bubonic plague. Since you seem to think you've got all the answers neatly sewn up, perhaps you'd like to explain that to me, Charles?"

At the unexpected sound of a sixth voice joining in the fray, Georgia's heart lurched with such joyful disbelief that she wondered how it remained fixed behind her ribs. Even overlaid with scourging anger, there was no mistaking that sexy drawl.

Swinging around, she fixed her gaze on the miraculous flesh and blood reality of Adam filling the entrance to the living room. Feet planted apart, thumbs hooked in the side pockets of black corduroy slacks, and two-day-old stubble smudging his jaw, he stood there oozing rage and sex appeal.

He looked travel-weary, furious and formidable. He looked absolutely, incredibly beautiful.

This was not how he had imagined coming back to her, with the whole gang forming a welcoming committee. In fact, when he'd turned in the driveway just in time to see her whole family trooping in through her front door, his first inclination had been to head the Rolls back to town and wait until tomorrow to announce his arrival. But throughout the long, arduous journey home to Piper Landing, he'd planned to surprise her with such anticipation that to be cheated at the last moment had left him feeling as disappointed as a kid who'd misread the calendar and woken up for Christmas a day early.

Intending to sneak upstairs and wait in her bedroom until they'd all gone home again, he'd quietly let himself in the front door just in time to hear the thoroughly married Samantha accuse, "It's Adam Cabot's baby, isn't it?"

It was the kind of announcement that tended to make a man forget everything he'd ever been taught about the ungentlemanly practice of eavesdropping. Without so much as a twinge of conscience, Adam had posted himself out of sight and brazenly absorbed every word of the ensuing debate.

He'd managed well enough to hold his peace, despite one startling revelation after another, until the man with the plummy voice had piped up again, at which point Adam had decided to ditch his original plan and make his presence known forthwith. It was almost worth it, just to see the looks on the assembled faces.

Natalie Chamberlaine gaped in a most unladylike manner, while a comically relieved expression rolled over her husband's face. Samantha turned an angry shade of puce and, clutching the arm of the twerp beside her, pointed and whispered, "That's him, Charles."

Charles, whose dapper three-piece suit and neatly trimmed mustach were so relentlessly correct that he couldn't possibly be anyone other than her husband, drew himself up to his full five-eight or whatever, and tried to look important.

Becomingly flushed and lusciously curved in all the right places, Georgia simply stared from her position by the window, her teal blue eyes so luminous with joy that, disapproving audience notwithstanding, Adam was hard-pressed not to sweep her into his arms and make good on all those erotic treats he'd promised himself during his lengthy absence.

The fact that he was considerably ticked off at her for calling a conference and divulging to her family news that he should have been the first to hear, cooled his ardor and helped him contain himself.

"Well?" He rocked back on his heels and surveyed the whole damned lot of them unsmilingly. "Isn't anyone going to answer my question? What's the difference?"

Samantha was the first to recover. "I'm married," she cawed sanctimoniously. "That's the difference in a nutshell, Adam Cabot."

"I'm sure you can understand our concern, Adam," the mother chipped in, for once at enough of a loss to sound uncommonly shaken. "Georgia has been through a terrible time in the last year or so. Her father and I think she's due for a little lasting happiness, for a change."

"It was never my intention to cause her unhappiness in the past, Mrs. Chamberlaine."

"I think I speak for everyone here when I say that it's your intentions for the future that interest us now," Charles of the plummy voice announced. "There's little doubt in my mind that you should be prepared to do the decent thing and marry her. You owe it to the family to spare them any further embarrassment. I know that if I were in your position—"

"You don't know diddly squat," Adam informed him with sublime impudence. "If you did, you'd get your fat hide out of here fast. Before I boot it out."

"Don't let him speak to you like that, Charles!" Samantha yelped.

"Adam...!" Georgia tried to look appalled but couldn't quite manage it due to the undimmed radiance of her smile.

Tempted to smile back, he scowled instead and looked away. He wasn't letting her off the hook that easily. She had a lot of explaining to do.

"Good to have you back, young man," her father murmured, ushering his wife to the door. "Come along, everyone. Adam is quite right, six is definitely a crowd. Good night, Georgia, my dear."

In the postscript of silence following their exit, she hovered by the window, leaving the next move up to him. The quiet glimmered between them with the expectancy of a bubble that, sooner or later, would grow too large to bear its own weight.

He was the one who finally punctured it. "Is it true, Georgia?" he asked, moving a step further into the room. "Are you really pregnant, or were you just stringing them along for the hell of it?"

"It's true," she said.

"And am I the father?"

Her smile wavered. "What sort of question is that, Adam? Of course you are!"

"Then how the hell come," he exploded softly, "am I the last to find out about it—again?"

This was not the homecoming she had envisaged. The first flash of glad reunion had evaporated somewhere between his announcing himself and her family's leaving.

"I had intended you to be the first. Samantha found out this morning quite by accident and took it upon herself to spread the news."

"And when did you find out, my darling?" There was nothing remotely tender in the way he tossed out the endearment.

Her determined confidence in a happy ending somewhat undermined by his attitude, she said hesitantly, "I knew for certain the day you left town again."

"That soon?" His gaze narrowed. "Then it must have happened—"

"That night at the chalet."

"You told me you'd seen a doctor, that you were protected."

"I know. I lied."

His voice grew chill. "And how do I know you're not lying now when you say I'm the father? How do I know it's not Steven's baby?"

"You could always ask him," she replied, anger flash-flooding through her. "For God's sake, Adam, you've been gone nearly two months and you haven't so much as bothered to say hello before you take over the inquisition where the rest of my family left off. If you can't, or won't believe me when I tell you you're the only man I've ever slept with, I'm not sure I want to hear anything else you might have to say, especially not if it's part of another little homily on trust."

That shook him. His gaze homed in on hers with burning intensity. "I do believe you," he muttered, raking a distracted hand through his hair. "Come here."

"No," she said. "You come to me. I'm tired of making all the concessions, of always being in the wrong. In fact, I'm just plain tired."

He crossed the room in two strides and pulled her into his arms. "Why didn't you say something before I left? I never would have gone if I'd known."

"Precisely. And I was no more prepared to use an unplanned pregnancy to hold you this time than I was before. Some things will never change, Adam. Either you came back of your own free will or I'd go on without you."

Gripping her by the shoulders, he held her away from him. "What are you saying?" he demanded. "That we're right back where we started last November?"

She filled her senses with his presence, drinking in the sight and texture of him. She'd been mistaken in believing she'd remembered him exactly as he was. Memory would always run a poor second to reality when it came to the long-lashed intensity of his blue eyes, the sensual curve of his mouth, the irreverent curl of his hair. And nothing but the living presence could ever convey the magnetic force of his personality. "No," she said, cupping his unshaven jaw in her hands. "This time I believed in you. I trusted you to come back to me as soon as you could. I believed you loved me as much as I love you. Now may I please be kissed?"

His mouth came down on hers, warm and ardent. "I never dreamed I'd miss you so much," he said, when they both came up for air. "You were in my mind every minute. I thought I'd go nuts when I was slogging through the snow-blown wilderness and had no way of keeping in touch with you. I must've asked myself a hundred times a day what the hell I thought I was doing, putting thousands of miles between us when all I wanted was to be by your side."

"You were a man with a mission," she said. "You had a debt to repay. How did it go?"

"I don't want to talk about it right now. I don't want to talk about anything. I didn't travel nonstop for three days to get back to you so that we could indulge in an all-night gabfest. I had something else in mind." He hooked his forefinger inside the collar of the high-necked, long-sleeved jumpsuit she wore. "What is this thing, a chastity shroud designed to keep a man frothing at the mouth as he tries to figure out his way inside it?"

"It's an original creation from an international fashion house and the designer would be dreadfully upset to hear it referred to as a shroud."

"I'm going to be dreadfully upset in another minute," Adam warned her, his sexy drawl inciting her to delicious anticipation. "It's been far too long since I made love to you and I'm in no mood to be thwarted now. In fact, I'm approaching such a dangerously high level of frustration that I just might rip the damned thing apart unless I find out how to strip it off in a more civilized fashion."

The unbridled passion smoking in his eyes left her weak at the knees. "In that case," she whispered, swaying against him, "there's a full-length zipper built into the back seam."

The words had scarcely cooled on her lips before the heavy jersey silk whispered around her ankles. "You feel different," he decided huskily, his hands and mouth charting her body with fatal tenderness. "You feel fuller and rounder and fabulously fecund."

She choked with laughter. "I've gained only four pounds. Your child has cost me breakfast every day for the last six weeks."

"Little brute," he murmured, swinging her into his arms and heading for the stairs. "I'm the only one allowed to cause you that sort of grief."

But over the next two hours he brought her such an abundance of pleasure and happiness that she decided all the long months of loneliness and despair had been worth it, especially when, just before they fell asleep, he promised, "I love you, Georgia. I will never leave you again."

\* \* \*

As Georgia had foreseen, her mother and sister lost no time following up on their unscheduled visit of the night before. With all the zeal of bloodhounds on the scent, they showed up at her studio the next morning minutes after she arrived there herself.

"So," Natalie asked expectantly, "do you know when you're getting married?"

"Not exactly," Georgia said, poising silver needle-nosed tweezers over the twelve small diamonds and a rare three-carat yellow sapphire lying on the black velvet pad in front of her.

Samantha huffed ominously. "That doesn't sound exactly promising. But then, Mother and I could've told you he'd balk when it came right down to proposing, couldn't we, Mother?"

"Oh, he proposed," Georgia said, taking wicked delight in teasing the pair of them. "We just haven't finalized the details, that's all. We might have got around to them this morning, but Adam had other business to attend to first."

Her mother looked apprehensive. "What's more important than setting a wedding date, dear—especially given the circumstances? Time isn't exactly on your side, you know."

"For a start, buying the privately owned Piper Landing TV station which recently came on the market. Now that he's officially out of the military, Mother, he has to find something else to do with his time."

"...besides," as he'd pointed out that morning over breakfast in bed, "making love to you night and day, that is."

"Buy the Piper Landing TV station?" Samantha gave an unladylike snort. "Oh, for heaven's sake, Georgia, don't tell me Adam plans to step in as local news anchorman? It takes more than flashy good looks to do a job like that, you know.''

"Yes,'' Georgia said, kindly refraining from pointing out that when it came to good looks, flashy or otherwise, Samantha hardly qualified as an expert if her husband exemplified her idea of male beauty. Charles was many things, but handsome was not one of them. "And fortunately, Adam has plenty more to offer.''

"I want to initiate a kind of televised correspondence school," he'd confided, securing a towel round his waist after his shower and lathering his jaw. "Something that covers the whole spectrum of post-secondary opportunities from trades to professions. The basic program's already in place, I know, but I want to take it further, make it more a sort of information channel that brings the rest of the world to people who can't discover it firsthand for themselves. I realized when I was trying to get Ikut settled up north that he's not alone in being isolated from opportunity. There are people living in some pretty remote areas in B.C. as well, and Piper Landing is ideally situated to provide them with this kind of service.''

"It sounds like a wonderful idea,'' Georgia had said, "but will it keep you busy enough?''

"Probably not, but I've also been offered a consultant position with a commercial aircraft company, a job I can do from here with only an occasional trip out of town. I've got a lot of technological expertise that isn't classified as privileged information. Then there are Bev's holdings, which she's been begging me to manage ever since I came back on the scene so that she can devote all her time to what she calls her 'recreational endeavors'.''

Georgia had ogled him through the mirror. "Will there be any time left over for other things?'' she'd teased.

"Like this, you mean?" he'd replied, flinging off the towel and nuzzling her with his soap-lathered jaw. "Always."

"Should we assume, from the sappy smile on your face, that you've got a pretty good idea of when you will get married?" Samantha inquired.

"Yes." With her tweezers, Georgia made a minor adjustment in her design, shifting the diamonds into closer alignment with the yellow sapphire. "We've narrowed it down to sometime a week from Saturday."

As she'd expected, that small tidbit of news sent her mother and sister into a complete flap.

"A week from Saturday?" Natalie yelped, gathering up purse and gloves. "Then why are we sitting here as if we have all the time in the world?"

"I have a business to run," Georgia pointed out. "I can't just close shop any time I feel like it."

"Leave everything to me, dear." Her mother squared her shoulders with the fortitude of one about to face a firing squad. "Not only is it my right as mother of the bride to take care of all the details, but, with both my girls in a delicate condition, it is also my duty. Heaven forbid either of you should endanger your health at such a time."

"You'll need my advice," Samantha informed her. "You know you'll forget something crucial, otherwise."

"I'll accept your help with gratitude," her mother countered. "Collect your gloves and let's get started. We have a wedding to organize."

"A shotgun wedding no less," Samantha mourned. "What will people think?"

"I really don't care," Natalie said. "I'm about to become a grandmother twice over and quite frankly what other people think about the timing isn't at the top of my list of priorities right now."

# CHAPTER ELEVEN

"YOUR MOTHER said that?" Adam asked incredulously over lunch at the Riverside Club. "I don't believe it."

"I think she's decided she quite likes you. Now, if we can just persuade Sam to give you a second chance..."

"It's how you feel about me that matters," he said, leaning over to plant a kiss on her mouth in full view of everyone else in the dining room. "By the way, I saw Steven when I was in the bank this morning."

"Oh." Georgia put down her fork, her appetite diminished by the guilt that washed over her at the knowledge that her present happiness had been acquired at Steven's expense. "Did you tell him—about us?"

"Yes. Everything, including the baby. I felt it was the least I could do. We've been friends for too long for me to let him find out some other way."

"How did he seem to take the news?"

"Surprisingly well. In fact, he'd like to extend his best wishes to you in person, so I invited him to join us here tonight for a drink before we go over to Bev's for dinner."

"I see."

Adam covered her hand with his. "Do you mind, Georgia?"

She shook her head. "Of course not. I just wish he could find someone and be as happy as we are."

"Maybe he already has. We didn't have a lot of time to talk earlier, but I got the impression that he wasn't too surprised when things didn't work out between you and him. He's getting on with his life, sweet pea, and unless I'm mistaken, it includes spending quite a bit of time with the new Personal Loans Manager working in the office next to his—and I don't mean spending time in a business sense.''

"If that's true, it would be the best wedding present in the world for me," Georgia said.

Without warning, Natalie descended on them, waving a sheet of paper in the air. "Hello, children, I thought I'd find you here. Sorry to interrupt your lunch, but I wanted to bring you up to date on the wedding plans."

"Sit down and join us for coffee," Adam invited, holding out a chair.

"I'll sit just for a moment, but no coffee, thank you, Adam. I really can't spare the time. Now, I practically had to go down on bended knee and beg, but I've persuaded Victor from the Mansion On The Bluff to close his restaurant for the day and let us hold the reception there because, of course, the Riverside Club has been booked for months, as has the Royal Landing Hotel. But never mind, the Mansion's a charming spot—a lovely old house with that gracious dining room which easily seats sixty. You did say you wanted to keep the guest list small, didn't you, Georgia?"

*Sixty*? Georgia nodded faintly, her visions of twenty or so guests evaporating. "Yes, Mother, small is what I had in mind."

"Good." Natalie ran a smart red fingernail down her list. "The church is booked for one in the afternoon with the reception to follow immediately after—not as chic a time as late afternoon or evening, I'm afraid, but I had to take what was available—and Caroline from the Bridal Aisle has a couple of gowns set aside for you to try because she sold the one you'd ordered for your last wedding, not that you'd want to wear it even if you could still get in it and—oh dear! Am I being terribly tactless?"

"Not at all," Adam assured her dryly. "But you're right, you don't need coffee. You're wired enough without it."

To Georgia's amazement, her mother giggled almost girlishly. "It's called running on nervous energy, my dear," she said, with the most warmth she'd ever exhibited toward Adam. "Now, Georgia, when can you stop by Caroline's and try on gowns?"

Georgia felt as though she'd accidentally stepped on a merry-go-round that was spinning out of control. After months of limbo, everything was happening a little too fast. "Tomorrow, maybe?"

"Good Lord, no!" Her mother looked aghast. "It has to be today, in case alterations are required and so that we can coordinate Samantha's dress. She *will* be your matron-of-honor, won't she?"

"I really hadn't envisaged anything quite so elaborate, Mother."

"I had," Adam said. "I want to make the most of your wedding day, sweet pea, because I don't intend for you to get the chance to do it over again. This marriage is for keeps." He smiled winningly at Natalie who beamed back at him as if she couldn't have come up with a better son-in-law had she gone out and snagged one herself. "Take her with you now, Mrs. Chamberlaine, and I'll hold down the fort at the studio."

"You don't know anything about jewelry," Georgia objected.

"I don't have to, to hang a Closed sign on the door." He kissed her again. "Go with your mother and have fun. Take all afternoon if you need to, as long as you leave enough time to put your feet up for an hour before we go out again tonight."

*    *    *

It was the start of a frantic race against time. Everyone joined in, rushing from one task to another. In the midst of the madness, Georgia and Adam maintained a little pool of calm and went about the more important business of rediscovering their pleasure in each other.

While everyone else talked flowers and champagne and caviar, she craved bananas and celery—preferably together. While her mother and Samantha watched her waistline as if they feared it might explode momentarily, Adam rested his head on her abdomen and told his unborn child how much he loved its mother. While her friends wanted bridal showers and teas and hoopla, she wanted to lie in bed with Adam and make love by moonlight.

Even Beverley was cordial, her beloved grandson's resurrection from the dead seeming to have mellowed her former disapproval of their relationship. "This is cause for celebration, grandchildren of mine," she caroled, descending on them in a cloud of purple chiffon and Jessica McClintock perfume the night Adam took Georgia over to the Walsh mansion to celebrate their renewed engagement. "You've been blessed by the Almighty and given a second chance. Adam, I do believe I'll forego my usual vodka for champagne."

Later, between puffs on her Russian Sobrani cigarette, she eyed Georgia speculatively. "You're not quite your usual sylphlike self, child. Is there, perhaps, another reason for the haste with which this wedding is being put together—apart from the fact that you and my grandson obviously can't live without each other, that is?"

"Well..." Georgia felt herself turn several shades of pink.

"Yes," Adam said. "She's pregnant."

"In that case, dear boy, may I suggest you lock your-selves in a closet until it's time to leave for the church, just to avoid the possibility of another tedious post-ponement? I do not fancy a great-grandchild of mine bearing the stigma of illegitimacy."

"There will be no more delays," Adam said. "You can count on that. Nothing is going to go wrong this time."

Georgia believed him. Was so intoxicated with hap-piness, in fact, that she agreed to several things that might have given her pause, had she been less elated. First, she moved in with her parents for the last few days before the wedding, "because," her mother argued per-suasively, "although I know you and Adam don't have a lot of use for doing things the traditional way, it would mean so much to your father to have you to leave as a bride from your old home, and I would love to spend this time sharing all those mother and daughter customs that make weddings so special."

Not to be outdone, Samantha planned a little dinner party. "Charles and I thought the evening before the wedding would be a good time," she announced, in the sort of *grande dame* manner guaranteed to provoke. "Of course, we'll invite your grandmother, Adam, and try to make it a true family affair."

"Very noble of you, Sammie, I'm sure," he replied pleasantly enough, adding in a wicked aside that only Georgia heard, "Want to bet she'll have our food poisoned?"

Then, with only seventy-two hours left before the cer-emony, Adam was called to Vancouver for an urgent meeting with Skylark Aeronautics, the company who'd hired him as a consultant.

"Afraid not," he said, when Georgia asked if business couldn't wait until after the wedding, "but don't worry, sweet pea, we'll be back in plenty of time for Sammie's dinner party. We'll fly out tomorrow morning and get the six o'clock flight home on Friday."

"We?" Samantha fumed, when she heard. "You mean to tell me you let him go roaming around on the loose in Vancouver with one of his Air Force cronies? You must be mad!"

"I'm his fiancée, not his keeper," Georgia snapped, a little edgy herself. "Furthermore, he's with his grandmother who has some last-minute shopping to take care of, so I hardly think there's any cause to worry that he'll go looking for trouble."

"Adam Cabot doesn't have to go looking," Samantha predicted dourly. "It finds him regardless."

She was right. Seven o'clock on Friday came and went with no sign of Adam. Then, just when Charles had decreed that they shouldn't hold dinner a moment longer, Georgia was called to the phone.

"Afraid we've hit a bit of a snag," Adam told her and she didn't need to hear what came next to know that he was calling long distance. "We missed our flight—"

"Adam!" She couldn't help the dismay that she knew filled her voice. "There isn't another until tomorrow afternoon, and we're supposed to be getting married at one."

"I haven't forgotten, sweetheart. As soon as I sort things out here, I'll rent a car and drive back. I can't say when I'll get in, but I'll be at the church on time, come hell or high water."

Georgia was not a superstitious person. She prided herself on her common sense and refused to allow her life to be governed by the random presence of black cats or ladders or any other manifestation of ill luck. But presentiment crawled over her skin with the creeping horror of insect feet. "Adam, what's happened?"

"Nothing for you to be concerned about," he said, but his tone belied the confidence in his words. "Look, I've got to go, I'm being paged. Apologize to Sammie for me and—" She heard him sigh. "—trust me, okay?"

She swallowed, ashamed of the doubts crowding her mind but unable to dismiss them. "Of course. I'm having a last-minute attack of bridal nerves, that's all. I'll see you tomorrow."

"At the church, if not before."

Common sense be damned! "*Not* before—it's bad luck!"

"Right." Again that sigh. "Let's not tempt Fate then. I love you, Georgia."

If there'd been a hint of softening in her family's attitude toward Adam in recent days, it evaporated when Georgia returned to the private dining room and relayed the news. "I could have told you something like this would happen," Samantha moaned. "My God, Georgia, he's going to stand you up at the last minute."

"No, he's not," Georgia said.

"The man's a bounder," Charles huffed, viciously spearing the olive in his predinner martini. "Plays fast and loose with a woman, gets her pregnant, and then pulls a stunt like this. You're better off without him, if you ask me."

"I'm not asking you," Georgia said.

"Darling," her mother began, shredding a perfectly manicured fingernail.

"Don't you start, too, Mother," she said. "I really don't need another load of doom and gloom right now. What I would like, very much, is for us all to have a pleasant dinner. Tomorrow is the day I marry the man I love and if you can't bring yourselves to approve of my choice, will you at least save your criticisms for when I'm not around to hear them?''

To give them credit, everyone tried, but the buoyant mood was gone, deflated by old doubts, wild imaginings and gloomy suspicions. When Georgia returned from the ladies' room in time to hear Charles remark, ''He wouldn't be the first man to pull a sneaky disappearing act at the eleventh hour,'' there seemed little point in perpetuating the charade of one big happy family having a whale of a good time.

''Adam isn't the sneaking kind,'' Georgia informed her brother-in-law wearily. ''He's the most forthright man I know which is probably why you all dislike him so much.''

''It's not that we dislike him,'' Natalie cried, springing up and flinging her arms around Georgia. ''It's that we love you, darling, and we're terribly afraid he's going to let you down.''

Surprisingly, Samantha hugged her, too. ''We want you to be happy, Georgia. It's all we've ever wanted. But things have happened so quickly—why, here it is, the eve of a wedding that, two weeks ago, none of us had any idea would be taking place—and everyone's present and accounted for but the groom.''

*Trust me*, Adam had said, and she would, because it was all she had to get her through the next few hours. ''Everything's going to work out,'' she told them. ''Please, everyone, just stop worrying, go home and get a good night's sleep. In another couple of hours, it'll be my wedding day.''

Early March in Piper Landing was usually lovely; mild, sunny, fragrant. However, it had been raining when Georgia awoke the next morning but she'd adamantly refused to admit to her mind the idea that anything could spoil this day. Nothing was going to go wrong, not even the weather.

"Oh, dear," her mother had murmured, joining her in the dining room and glancing outside at the clouds racing across the sky.

"It will clear up by noon," Georgia had insisted, opening the window and leaning out to inhale the heady scent of damp earth and hyacinths just as Samantha's car turned in the driveway.

"I hope so," Natalie said. "After all, 'happy the bride the sun shines on', you know."

"I'm going to be a happy bride even if it snows, Mother."

"I do admire your spirit, darling. Come and eat a little breakfast now, before the hairdresser gets here. It's after nine already."

"Aren't you going to join me?"

"No." Her mother had shuddered delicately. "I couldn't eat a thing. I'm too worried that...did Adam say when he expected to get back?"

"No." Georgia had helped herself to a Belgian waffle heaped with strawberries Romanoff, deeply grateful that her morning sickness had disappeared. "I thought I felt the baby move during the night. Do you think that's possible so soon?"

"Well, you are fourteen weeks along." Natalie, who'd been pouring coffee, suddenly had set down the pot and started to weep helplessly. "Oh, Georgia, I never thought it would be like this...all uncertain and back to front and you not being able to fit into your dress. I always saw you as the radiant, picture-perfect bride."

"I'll still be radiant," Georgia had said softly.

"But will you be a bride, darling?"

"Yes, so please don't cry and try not to worry. Adam will be waiting when I get to the church. He promised me he would."

Her mother had dabbed at her eyes with a linen serviette. "And you believe him, do you?"

"If I didn't, I'd have no business marrying him, Mom."

"Oh, God!" Samantha had exclaimed from the doorway. "Now what's happened?"

"Nothing," Georgia had replied, determinedly serene. "Mother's exercising her prerogative to weep buckets all over the bride, that's all. What's that you've got, Sam?"

"A blue silk garter," Samantha had said, adding darkly, "and I'll throttle that man of yours with it if he lets anything happen to spoil this day."

Praying that her optimism would not fall victim to such manifest votes of nonconfidence, Georgia had fixed a smile on her face. "And if Charles gets out of hand, I'll return the favor."

Now, three hours later and draped in bridal satin and lace, she wondered how she'd managed to fool everyone for so long, even herself. There hadn't been a word from Adam and although she might look composed on the outside, inside she was a mess.

Natalie swept into the room, resplendent in orchid silk. "Here are Great-Grandmother Chamberlaine's diamonds," she said, holding out the antique teardrop earrings that every bride for generations had worn. "Something old and borrowed, darling."

"And you've got your garter for something blue and new," Samantha said.

Her father poked his head around the door. "The limousines have arrived, my dears. We should be leaving in a few minutes. My goodness, Georgia, you're a vision."

Samantha pressed the outsized bouquet of sweet peas and stephanotis into her hands. "Just remember to hold it so that people won't notice your bulge."

That sense of being trapped on a merry-go-round caught up with Georgia again. What if Adam wasn't waiting at the church? What if, next week at this time, she was right back where she'd been the year before? What if...?

"Come along, my dear." Her father's hand was firm on her elbow, guiding her down the stairs and out the front door.

"The sun is shining," her mother cried. "You were right, Georgia, it's going to be a lovely day, after all."

"Of course it is," Samantha said, and blew her nose noisily. "Good God, I do believe I'm going to cry. This is all that Adam Cabot's fault, Georgia."

Somehow, everything always came back to Adam. It had been that way from the moment she'd first set eyes on him. It would be like that for the rest of her life. Suddenly, Georgia knew a great sense of calm. "Make sure you tell him that, when we get to the church, Sam."

"Always assuming he's there," her sister said.

"He will be," Georgia said.

And he was. As was his grandmother. In a wheelchair.

"We were on our way to the airport, dear child, when our taxi was involved in a collision at a stop sign," she explained, looking like a gypsy in dangling gold earrings and a long, fringed shawl. "I have a badly sprained ankle, and I'm sorry to say your bridegroom suffered a slight concussion although he's quite recovered now and should not find himself at all impaired on the honeymoon. But those fools at the hospital didn't think he should drive and insisted on keeping him overnight, but he didn't want to tell you that when he phoned yesterday evening. We got back to town about an hour

ago—scarcely time to change into our wedding finery—
but I thought it unfair to expect you to promise to love,
honor and cherish a man without knowing the reason
he stood you up at dinner, so I decided to waylay you
before you started down the aisle. Now, kiss my cheek,
child, and get that nice young man over there to push
me to my rightful place in the front pew."

"The old bat!" Samantha muttered. "Trust her to try
to upstage the bride."

But Georgia didn't reply. All her attention was fo-
cused on Adam, who'd turned and impaled her in his
dark blue stare.

Something rolled over in Georgia's stomach. Not the
baby, but a wave of emotion made up of all those things
that spelled love between a man and a woman: tenderness and passion; trust and desire.

The organ rolled out its notes. The processional began.
Samantha swept forward, nodding graciously at the
guests, and took her place to the right of the altar. In
the front pew across the aisle from Beverley Walsh,
Natalie dabbed at her eyes with a lace handkerchief.

Georgia hitched up her bouquet to hide her bulge, and
took her father's arm. Everyone turned to watch but she
saw only Adam.

She'd covered three of the ten yards separating her
from him when his mouth twitched. Another yard, and
his eyes crinkled. Two more yards and he was grinning
that damnably sexy, irreverent grin. Four more yards—
eight steps—and she was beside him.

"What's so funny?" she hissed.

"I never saw a pregnant angel before," he whispered,
wrapping his fingers around hers. "Give that hothouse
garden to your matron of honor, my darling, so I can
say good morning to my baby, then let's get this show
on the road."

# Coming Next Month

HARLEQUIN PRESENTS®

## THE BEST HAS JUST GOTTEN BETTER!

**#1845 RELATIVE SINS Anne Mather**
Alex mustn't know Sara's secret. But her small son Ben adores
him and she has to admit that Alex is ideal father material....
Is the answer to keep it in the family?

**#1846 ANGRY DESIRE Charlotte Lamb**
**(SINS)**
Gabriella realized she couldn't marry Stephen and ran out on
him on their wedding day. But Stephen wouldn't take "I don't"
for an answer....

**#1847 RECKLESS CONDUCT Susan Napier**
**(9 to 5)**
Marcus Fox didn't approve of Harriet. She put it down to her
new bubbly blond image. Then Marcus reminded her of the
events at the last office party....

**#1848 THEIR WEDDING DAY Emma Darcy**
**(This Time, Forever)**
Once he was her boss, and her lover.... And now Keir is back in
Rowena's life. Can they let go of their past and forge a future
together?

**#1849 A KISS TO REMEMBER Miranda Lee**
**(Affairs to Remember)**
It was time for Angie to stop comparing every man she met with
Lance Sterling and move on. Here she was, twenty-four and a
virgin...and suddenly Lance was back in her life!

**#1850 FORSAKING ALL OTHERS Susanne McCarthy**
When Leo Ratcliffe proposed to Maddie, was he promising the
true love of which she'd always dreamed—or merely offering
a marriage for his convenience?

Harlequin brings you the best books, by the best authors!

# ANNE MATHER

"...her own special brand of enchantment."
—*Affaire de Coeur*

Watch for:
## #1845 RELATIVE SINS
## by Anne Mather

Sara has a secret that her brother-in-law, Alex, must
never know. But her small son, Ben, adores him. Sara
has to admit that Alex is ideal father material, but his
motives are a mystery to her. Is he playing a game to
which only he knows the rules?

Harlequin Presents—the best has just gotten better!
Available in November wherever
Harlequin books are sold.

# HARLEQUIN PRESENTS®

## by Charlotte Lamb

A compelling seven-part series

Coming next month:

The Sin of Anger
in
## #1846 ANGRY DESIRE

As she stared at her wedding dress, Gabriella realized
she couldn't go through with her wedding to Stephen.
The only way out was to run...but would Stephen
come looking for her...?

Love can conquer the deadliest of

Harlequin Presents—the best has just gotten better!
Available in November wherever
Harlequin books are sold.

SINS6